The Wall

by

John Cannell

© John Cannell 2007
Printed and bound in the UK by Biddles Limited, Kings' Lynn,
Norfolk
ISBN 978-0-9556449-0-0

Author's Note

It is customary to start a novel with a note denying any resemblance between people or places described in the following story. That is not the case with this one.

Firstly, the events of 1918/19: Ellen Willmott was of course a renowned botanist of the nineteenth and twentieth centuries. She was a character who begs to be written about. Jacob Maurer was in charge of her alpine garden, and James Robinson was her butler. The estate was more or less as described. Other characters and the story line itself exist only in my own mind.

As far as current events are concerned, although the individuals named are fictitious, there is indeed a band of good humoured and hard working volunteers who, under the dedicated control of a warden and an assistant warden, do their best to maintain Warley Place as a Wildlife Refuge. Since the Essex Naturalists' Trust (now the Essex Wildlife Trust) took over its management in 1977 the estate has been transformed from the jungle it had become. Paths have been cut out and marked, countless sycamores cut down, walls re-pointed and in some cases rebuilt; Giant hogweed, Japanese knotweed, Himalayan Balsam and other weeds have been eradicated and the plants that remained from the original garden encouraged to blossom and grow.

Genuine though the setting is, the story itself is of course just fiction - which is a shame, because one can really imagine it being true.

Warley Place as it stands is a magical place, full of mystery and history. There is no gift shop; there are no toilets, and only a bare minimum of way markers. That is why the general public are not encouraged to visit other than on organised public days, although Essex Wildlife Trust members are welcome at any time.

It is a place that is special to those who work there, none less than your author.

My thanks go to the chair of the Warley Place Management Committee, Fiona Agassiz, who kept pestering me to get it published; to my brother Derek and my wife Shirley, who spent time reading through the original draft to correct countless typos and other errors and also encouraged its publication; also my good friend Chris Darby who had the nerve to insist on a fairly major rewrite of the main characters to the great benefit of the story; finally to several of the volunteers who also made useful comments and gave me encouragement.

The book is dedicated to the volunteers of Warley Place.

1

The Mistress of Warley Place

'Gertrude Jekyll may have been right,' said Jacob Maurer to James Robinson as they stood by the conservatory at the rear of the big house. 'Ellen Willmott probably was the greatest woman gardener of her day. In fact as far as I am concerned she still is. But that doesn't mean she hasn't got eccentric and rather crabby in her old age. And as for the way she treats people, it's nineteen thirty-four for goodness' sake, the world's a different place now. She's still living in the nineteenth century.'

Jacob fiddled with his huge moustache. It made his already sad looking face even sadder but he wouldn't shave it off. Small in stature and quiet in nature he preferred the time when James Preece was in charge, leaving him to concentrate on his alpine garden. He had neither the appearance of a head gardener nor, if the truth were known, the inclination and did in fact prefer to work alone. The reverse was not the case however, the few staff left on the estate all vying for the chance to work with Jacob Maurer; there were none to equal him as far as alpine plants were concerned and he was always happy to pass on his hard won knowledge.

Looking after fifty-five acres of grounds was impossible and would have been so however good a manager he was, for he no longer had the staff to manage. The numbers had dwindled from a peak of about a hundred at one time to a mere handful now. Even the thirty-three acres remaining of the original Warley Place estate was far too much for the few men left and it was rapidly deteriorating into a jungle while they concentrated on a few select areas.

'It's all right for you,' said James Robinson. 'You're still young, not yet turned sixty, and you can lose yourself in your alpine garden. I'm seventy-three and at her beck and call all the time while she's in the house, which has been more and more lately. Where is she anyway?'

Robinson was a taller and more distinguished person, easy to talk to and with the ability to calm things down when trouble

1

loomed – which was a big asset in the current times. As her various so-called friends had deserted her at approximately the same rate as her fortunes dwindled he had become her close confidant rather than the butler he once was.

'Looking round the rockery I think. She hasn't been walking round much at all these last couple of weeks. She's not doing badly at all though for a rheumatic seventy-six year old. Actually I miss her not creeping up on me to see what I'm up to. It used to drive the men mad but I liked having someone who was interested in what I was doing and knowledgeable enough to argue with me about how to do it.'

'I suppose you wouldn't still be here if you didn't like her. How long is it now?'

'Forty years. It's been good, most of it. Where else would I have got the opportunity to build an alpine garden like hers?'

'I've been butler here for forty-four years. Eighteen-ninety I started. And yes, she's done well. I can moan about her to you Jacob because I know you feel the same as I do. For all her eccentricity and sharp remarks, she's a lovely person. She doesn't ask anyone to put up with what she wouldn't put up with herself.'

He waved his hand at the big house.

'Look at that, for instance. Library, Music Room, Chapel, Dining Room, Morning Room, sixteen bedrooms, God knows how many other rooms, and what does she do? She lives in one room with an oil stove! Her own dining room and she has bread and cheese for lunch!'

They were silent for a while, watching a robin scratching in the earth.

'What does she want us for anyway?' asked Jacob.

'I don't know. It's a bit unusual, I must say. You're gardens, I'm house. Neither of us can cope, that's about the only thing we have in common.'

'And that we are her two most loyal servants,' suggested Jacob.

'Loyal or not, we can't live on fresh air.'

'But at least if anything happens to her you'll still have a roof over your head,' said Jacob. 'I'll be thrown out of South Lodge with nowhere to go and if her finances are as bad as they seem to be then I'll have no pension either.'

'How on earth did it come to this?' asked Robinson. 'She built Warley Place up to something wonderful, now it's worse than when the Willmott family moved in. It might have been different had she married but who would have put up with her?'

They were quiet again for a bit. The robin had departed for a more fruitful area so they contented themselves with watching for Ellen Willmott's appearance at the conservatory door to usher them in.

'September is nearly over,' said Jacob, 'and so is summer. I like autumn though. I like spring better, but autumn is fine.'

Robinson consulted his pocket watch. 'It's six o'clock.'

'Oh dear, there's some balsam in the border,' said Jacob, fidgeting. 'I must at least clear it from the sight of the house even if it is rife elsewhere.'

'Things are difficult at the moment,' said Robinson.

Jacob took a few steps and pulled several of the yellow flowered weeds from the ground, stuffed them in his pocket and walked back to join his colleague.

'Whatever it's like for us, it must be ten times worse for her,' he said eventually. 'She's a wonderful person who has great talent and had plans to match. Extravagant, yes, but the war must have played havoc with her investments. There will never be another like her.'

'You are right there,' agreed Robinson. 'A wonderful person.'

'Not so wonderful,' said a high pitched voice behind them.

True to form, she had come back the long way round through the coach house and the walled garden, approaching them from the rear. They both knew that, suspicious as always, she wanted to hear what they were saying about her. After all these years of loyal service she still couldn't accept that these two people loved and respected her as they did.

Although not a pretty woman in the traditional feminine sense, she was striking in appearance. Even with her small, though by no means diminutive, stature she radiated authority by means of her piercing eyes and regal carriage, her advanced age notwithstanding. She had long since given up dressing to suit her position, but somehow the casual though sombre clothes advertised the fact that she did not need to enhance her natural authority by covering herself in fine linen.

3

'Come on in,' she said, opening the conservatory door and walking through. 'I'm hungry. Cheese and some of that nice bread James? No Jacob, no need to remove your boots, this floor has seen far worse.'

Jacob smiled to himself. If he had left them on she would have told him to remove them.

'My feet are aching,' he said. 'I have brought some shoes if you don't mind.'

By the time he had changed into more comfortable footwear Robinson had reappeared with a tray on which were heaped bread, butter, cheese, plates and knives; a jug of water and some glasses were already on the table. He unloaded the tray, put it aside and the three of them settled into their chairs.

'The estate is in a mess, isn't it,' she said as she buttered a thick slice of bread and cut some cheese. 'That is not a criticism of either of you, no-one could do more. It is just a statement of fact. What do you think?'

She would have given a sharp retort to any attempt at a denial, but neither of the two men wanted openly to agree with her, however true her statement might be.

'Well?'

'Things are difficult, it's true,' said Jacob eventually. 'The outer parts of the garden are indeed not easy to keep under control. Nature is a powerful enemy at times.'

She nodded and looked at Robinson.

'The house too needs much attention,' he said, reassured by her acceptance of Jacob's statement. 'But with few visitors now one has to question whether it is really of any importance.'

'Very tactfully put, both of you,' she said, 'if rather understated. The fact is that I have run out of money and can not afford to run Warley Place. But I don't know what to do. I am tired and no longer feel able to carry on the fight.'

'We have been through difficult times before,' said Robinson, 'and we have always come through in the end.'

'Surviving, that is all,' she said wearily. 'But things will never be what they were, I have to accept that. It is simply not fair for you two to do almost on your own what a hundred people once did. Not just unfair, impossible.'

The two were silent for a minute. They had never heard her like this before, accepting defeat. She had always denied that there was a problem at all, let alone that it might be insurmountable.

'We could simply let the outer reaches go,' suggested Jacob. 'Just make sure that the parts near the house are kept as you wish them.'

'Would you let your alpine garden go, Jacob? Could you or I bear to see it revert to a weed infested wilderness?'

Jacob shook his head.

'And you, James, could you just let this house rot away? It's no use, I will have to sell.'

'No!' they both cried.

'Maybe at some stage someone will bring the garden back to its former glory,' she continued, 'but for now we will have to let go. The years of depression are over, the future looks promising. Perhaps someone will pay well for it. If they do I will instruct them to keep you, Jacob, to manage the gardens. You, James, will no doubt wish to retire but perhaps you could stay to manage the changeover for the new owner.'

'What about you, Miss Ellen?' asked Jacob.

'I fear that I shall not survive the change for very long, but perhaps I shall end my days in one of the cottages doing my best not to interfere.'

'We have had some good times here,' said Robinson in an attempt to lighten the mood just a little. 'I have waited on the rich and famous, indeed on royalty. I have been left to run this house as I have wished, especially during your absences abroad. I would not have changed one single day of my life here.'

'And I have been able to oversee the development of the best alpine garden in Europe,' said Jacob. 'Nowhere else would I have had that opportunity. You have spared no expense in obtaining plants from all over the world. I too am glad to have had my time here, whatever may come.'

There was silence for a moment.

'Forgive me if I seem patronising,' continued Jacob. 'But perhaps best of all has been that I have worked alongside the great Ellen Willmott.'

'Amen to that,' said Robinson.

'Your kind words are not deserved,' murmured their mistress, her eyes misting.

Jacob swallowed the last of his cheese and sipped his water.

'Would you do anything different?' asked Robinson.

'I have been too extravagant and would have been less so if it would have saved Warley Place,' she said, staring out through the conservatory window. 'But more than that, I wish there were four of us here this evening.'

Jacob glanced quickly at Robinson, who was used to his mistress's strange comments but who was nevertheless looking more than a little puzzled.

'Me too,' said Jacob, understanding only too well what she meant. 'Me too.'

'I would like to thank you for all you have done,' she said, changing the subject abruptly as if annoyed at her uncharacteristic show of sentimentality. 'It has been a privilege to have you both working for me. Now I am a little tired and wish to retire early.'

The two men rose to their feet and Jacob walked to the door.

'Jacob,' said Ellen Willmott, following him.

He turned to her.

'Thank you,' she said, and to his amazement kissed him on both cheeks.

He knew exactly to what she was referring and nodded, feeling his own eyes moistening and his throat tightening. She gave him a comforting smile and let him pick up his boots and continue on his way.

'Can I help, Miss Ellen?' asked Robinson as Jacob trudged his way back to South Lodge.

'No, I will be fine. I have a little indigestion but nothing more. I would like to retire to my room now.'

She slowly made her way upstairs. Tired though she was, she slept badly that night and before dawn broke properly she rose, restless and ill at ease. Going to the window she could see the trees emerging out of the early morning mist and the glow from the sun before it showed itself above the horizon. The beauty of the scene and the sound of the birds welcoming the dawn did nothing to lift her spirits.

She brought up a little wind. That was the trouble with eating cheese before going to bed. She even felt a little nauseous.

'I can never leave this place,' she said. 'Never.'

She started to sweat and clutched at the window sill to avoid falling.

She gasped as the indigestion tightened across her chest.

'Now I'll never have to,' she murmured to herself in sudden grateful realisation as the pain travelled down one arm. 'Perhaps there is a God.'

She crumpled to the floor.

The Mistress of Warley Place was dead.

2

Donald

Donald settled back and picked up his book. A biography of Isambard Kingdom Brunel: architect, surveyor and above all engineer, all rolled into one. It was the engineering Brunel was famous for of course. Railways, bridges, ships, tunnels, he designed them all. There was a time, too many years ago, when Donald had similar dreams but his engineering career had risen only to leading a modest team working on similarly modest projects. Now he had retired and it was too late.

Pushing those thoughts aside he ran his fingers over the smooth surface of the dust jacket and eased back the cover.

Perhaps if he had worked just a bit harder at university or in the office things might have been different. But his life hadn't been too bad, had it? The job had been quite interesting, most of the time, and his family life had been all right.

He reached the bottom of the page, went to turn it over and realised he couldn't remember what he had just read. Starting again, he got half way through before putting it down with a sigh.

Sunday mornings were boring. Well actually quite a lot of the mornings were boring, now he came to think about it. And the afternoons were not much better. He got up and walked into the kitchen. Susan was in the garden pottering about with her plants. Married to her for forty years and much though he liked looking at them he still hadn't got the hang of which flower was which. She was lucky having a hobby.

He turned, caught sight of his reflection in the window of the kitchen unit and shuddered. Not tall, but not short; a little overweight, but not grossly so; hair still mostly dark but showing signs of thinning but nothing more than one would expect from someone of his age. Actually more than just showing signs of thinning if you looked at the back, which is why he never did. Pretty average. That summed him up. A good epitaph, he thought. 'Here lies Donald Johnson, Pretty Average.'

He wandered into the garden and stood quietly watching his wife deftly easing weeds from between her pansies. He knew pansies, they were easy. Sensing his presence, she turned and looked up.

'Oh dear,' she said. 'Have you been thinking again?'

'No,' he protested. Then, 'Well, actually, just a bit.'

'Come on,' she said, grimacing a little as she got to her feet. 'We're going out.'

'No, I only came out here to stretch my legs. I was just starting my book.'

'It will do you good.'

'Oh dear, now I feel guilty. I've stopped you from working.'

'Come on, the weather is just right.'

'Where?'

'Warley Place.'

'Oh. Isn't that the place out past Warley, by that pub?'

'The *Thatcher's Arms*. That's right. Doreen was saying it was worth a visit, so now is as good a time as any.'

'I don't really feel like it at the moment. Perhaps later.'

Susan took a deep breath, turned, knelt down and got on with her weeding.

'Well if you want to go....'

'No, I don't particularly want to go. I've got plenty to do here.'

'I'll just pop to the shops and get a paper then.'

He turned and made his way back into the house. Best to walk away when she was in that sort of mood, he always thought.

He shut the front door quietly, in case she thought he was in a huff, walked quickly down the path and turned right towards the high road. Warley Place indeed, just because Doreen said so. He'd spent his life doing what other people told him and he wasn't going to put up with people like Doreen carrying on where his boss had left off.

He'd looked forward to retirement. To doing just what he wanted to, when he wanted to. Trouble was, he wasn't sure what that was. He'd been looking forward to reading about Brunel, now he wasn't even doing that.

Brentwood was boring; a typical London dormitory town. A main street, usually teeming with cars and lorries, nose to tail, all in a desperate hurry to get who knows where. A few dozen shops each side of this stream of metal, surrounded by thousands of houses. Occupied by fifty thousand people or more, all of whom wanted to walk on the same side of the street as you, pushing and shoving, too preoccupied with their own business even to notice you.

Except on Sundays. Then the place was dead. Worn out by their week of rushing about they stayed in bed, or mowed the lawn, or went to church, or the Sainsbury's supermarket, generally preparing themselves for another frenetic week ahead. But not him. Now he had retired, frenetic weeks were a thing of the past. He needed a purpose in life. And not continually decorating the house, that wasn't a purpose in life, that was a sentence. 'You will be taken from here to a place where you will decorate your house until you are dead,' he visualised the judge saying, after placing the black cap on his head. Not that Susan had asked him to redecorate, he had to admit that. But she probably did want him to.

He reached the High Street, walked along a few yards and turned to cross the road to the paper shop. A car blasted him with its horn and he jumped back on to the pavement, feeling the adrenaline flow. 'Stupid idiot,' he hissed after the driver, who was shaking his head.

With nothing else in sight, he crossed with exaggerated care and stopped at the camera shop, looking at the gleaming equipment in the window. Perhaps he could get himself a really good camera and take up photography as a hobby. Yes, that would probably be good. Then he could take pictures of, well, almost anything, and perhaps even print them himself. Pentax, Canon, Nikon, they all looked the same to him.

Suddenly realising that he wasn't sure how long he had been staring at the window he turned, crossed the road and made his way back home. Passing the rows of anonymous houses that led down to their own anonymous tree-lined road, he wondered what they did each weekend. Old Bob Evans, he watched sport on the TV most of the time. How boring. Tim worked in his garden whatever the weather but Susan did theirs so that was out. He wasn't sure what the others did.

Home already. He put his key in the latch and opened the door. Susan had come in from the garden and was making some tea.

'Hello dear,' she said as he walked in. 'No paper?'

3

In which Charles relaxes before going back to the Front

'Thank you for another lovely meal Sir James,' said Charles, his hand rubbing his stomach. 'And to you, Lady Mary. It's been a real pleasure coming here again. It always is.'

'My goodness young feller, I've told you before it's James and Mary,' said his prospective father-in-law. 'And the pleasure is all ours. Eh, my dear?'

'It certainly is,' said his wife.

Charles smiled. He really did enjoy these visits. Not only to get away from the dreadful war for a bit, but for the genuinely delightful company. He'd been very apprehensive indeed when Harry had invited him to stay during their first visit home on leave from France, having already been told about his father's knighthood and the huge estate on which they lived. Harry could be very persuasive when he wanted and Charles relented in the end. That was when he met Harry's sister Olivia and experienced what he had often pooh-poohed; love at first sight.

'Pity you can't stay longer,' continued Sir James. 'I've told you before, I could put in a word you know.'

'No Pa,' said Harry. 'We've got to do our bit. Back to the Front tomorrow, both of us.'

Funny, thought Charles, how before meeting Harry and his family he had thought of the upper class as either very intimidating or alternatively boring and frankly a bit stupid, living on their easy money, reputation and connections in the right places. That might be the case with some, but it certainly wasn't true of this family. Harry was his best friend in the squadron in France, popular despite his dashing good looks and obvious ancestry.

'That's right,' confirmed Charles. 'We leave at mid day tomorrow.'

'No chance of joining us in bagging a few birds in the morning then?'

11

'I think we'll be doing enough shooting when we get back to France,' said Harry.

Sir James frowned as Lady Mary put her handkerchief to her mouth, her eyes wide. 'Quite, quite.'

'But it's nearly over now, isn't it?' Olivia pleaded. 'It's been four years. Nineteen-eighteen should see the end not only to this war, but all wars. I read that in *The Times* last week.'

'Oh yes, we've got them on the run now,' grunted Sir James. 'Our men are superior and we're getting some decent equipment at last. I gather the Handley Page drops sixteen one-hundredweight bombs at one go. They don't stand a chance.'

What's with all this 'we' stuff, wondered Charles. And their guns seem every bit as lethal as our guns, their aeroplanes every bit as fast and manoeuvrable.

'It's good to be able to take the offensive in the air after the damage they've done to us with their Zeppelins and Gothas,' Charles agreed.

'Oh yes, bombing civilians, what on earth is the world coming to. Can't expect any better from the Hun though I suppose. What are you flying now son?' Sir James directed his question to Harry, sitting quietly fiddling with his napkin.

'Probably still the F.E.2d. Getting a bit old now, but it can drop a fair load of bombs on the enemy and the other chap can carry out useful observation when he's not firing his gun. They might let me have a Sopwith, like Charles. Bit lonely on your own though, and you can't really fly the thing and take decent photographs at the same time. There was some talk of a Bristol Fighter. That would be far better than the F.E.2. – all the advantages of two seats but the performance of a single seater.'

Harry had a relaxing way of talking that could put people at ease in seconds, but Charles wondered if the others could see the slightly too wide-open eyes, the licking of dry lips, the hands now clenched, the rigid body that he was trying hard to hide. Perhaps he could only recognise the signs himself because he too was frightened of death, and especially of mutilation. But the one thing they were both even more frightened of was being seen as cowards.

'I prefer a single-seater,' said Charles, rescuing his friend. 'Then you've only got yourself to worry about. And the Camel's not a bad kite. Faster than the old Pup and with my two guns they don't stand a chance once you get them in your sights.'

'You'll have something else to think about soon though!' said Sir James good-naturedly, glancing at Olivia.

Lady Mary put her hand on her husband's. 'Oh yes, we're all so looking forward to the wedding,'

'Can we change the subject?' Olivia said, blushing slightly.

She really was beautiful, thought Charles as he smiled at her. Long black hair framing a perfectly shaped oval face, nice full lips, slim body with firm inviting breasts. Whatever did she see in him, with his nondescript brown hair, several inches below Harry's six foot, slightly over weight, and adequate but undistinguished background? He was a very lucky man.

'Music?' suggested Lady Mary.

They rose from the table and made their way across the hall to the music room at the rear of the house. If someone had ever told him that he would marry someone who lived in a house with its own music room he would have thought they were mad. I wonder if Olivia will miss this opulence, he wondered. Or perhaps Daddy will make sure she has what she wants. He'd certainly made it clear that he'd welcome them staying there, in their own apartment of course. Oh well, worry about that after the war.

'Let's get away if we can,' whispered Olivia as Lady Mary sorted through some music. 'We can go down to the lake.'

'*The Rose* would be good tonight I think,' said her mother, holding some music aloft.

'Oh mother, I really don't feel like singing tonight,' pleaded Olivia.

'Just the one, then you and Charles can be on your own for a bit,' she said smiling. 'I know that's what you want.'

'Thank you Lady Mary – sorry, Mary – we'd like to have a few minutes at some stage, but it is my favourite.' He turned to Olivia. 'I'd dearly love to hear you sing it one more time before I go back.'

He settled himself behind the piano while Olivia stood by his side and Harry put his violin to his shoulder.

Charles didn't need to look at the music, none of them did, they had performed it so often. The haunting introduction, with each instrument dancing softly with the other, led at last into Olivia's rich mezzo-soprano voice.

'Tis the last rose of summer,' she sang.
'Left blooming all alone,'
The beauty of her singing never failed to move him.
'All her lovely companions ,
Are faded and gone.'
Her voice effortlessly trickled up and down the scale like a waterfall into a still pool.
'No flower of her kindred,
No rose bud is nigh,'
No full soprano could sound as good as this.
'To reflect back her blushes,
Or give sigh for sigh.'

They looked to Sir James, who normally came in with his deep baritone voice for the repetition of the verse, but he shook his head. Charles could see tears in his eyes and felt his own start to water. Why couldn't it always be like this?

Not wanting to embarrass him, Charles carried on playing but joined in the singing himself the second time round. He was relieved to hear the deep slightly off-key voice of his future father-in-law join in for the last line.

'To reflect back her blushes,
Or give sigh for sigh.'

As the last notes faded away there was one of those silences that indicates an audience's sorrow that an extraordinary performance has finished and a desire to hear the very last echoes even if they are only in one's head.

'Never heard it sung or played better,' said Sir James finally as they applauded each other. 'Until I joined in, that is, what!'

'You have a lovely voice dear,' said Lady Mary, the rest nodding in agreement.

'One day we'll have to sing the whole three verses instead of repeating the first,' Charles said to nobody in particular.

'We'll have to learn the words first!' laughed Harry.

'They are rather sad,' broke in Olivia, 'So I'd rather give them a miss. I'd like a spot of fresh air before the sun goes down.'

'Me too,' agreed Charles, immediately noticing Sir James' frown.

'Can I join you?' asked Harry. 'I'd like a last look round too before we go back.'

'Jolly good idea,' said Sir James. For a moment Charles thought he might be joining them too, but happy that there was now a chaperone he settled back into his chair and reached for the cigars.

'Don't worry old boy,' whispered Harry while Olivia went for a wrap, knowing the temperature would fall when the sun went down. 'I'll leave you two alone when we're out of sight.'

'No need,' Charles started to protest, somewhat half-heartedly.

'I'm only coming because Pa wanted me to keep an eye on you. Anyway, I want to see if the badgers come out tonight.'

They turned to greet Olivia.

'You always look stunning,' said Charles, his heart melting. 'But tonight you look particularly so.'

'See you later Pa,' said Harry. 'Don't worry if we are a little late, we might see if the badgers are out. It's a lovely warm evening, we might as well make the most of it.'

'Well, not too late then.'

They walked out through the big door into the evening, standing for a moment on the steps leading down to the front lawns and garden, the elm avenue to the lake beyond with the forest to either side.

'To the lake?' suggested Harry.

'To the lake,' agreed Charles, looking down to check if Olivia had changed into sensible walking shoes – which she had.

She smiled at him and linking one of her arms with his and the other with Harry's, she ushered them on.

They walked in silence for a while, thoughts unspoken.

'Let's go through the trees,' she said finally as they came to a choice between that or the long straight path to the lake.

'So Pa won't be able to see us?' grinned Harry.

'Can't get into trouble with you here,' said Olivia ruefully.

'Don't worry, I really am going to look at my badgers. We're out of sight now. You know where they are Liv, just over there. Collect me on the way back – and don't make it too late, you heard what the old man said. Don't want him out here looking for us!'

'Harry,' called Olivia as he walked off.

'Yes?'

15

'Thank you.'

He waved his arm and made his way off the path and through the trees to a grassy bank. They saw him settle himself down for the evening and with a final wave they continued down the path.

'He's a fantastic friend,' said Charles. 'I'd go mad without him in France. I can open up to him in a way I couldn't with anyone else. I think he can with me.'

'Yes, he can. He's often said so.' Then after a pause. 'He's frightened, isn't he? Beneath all that casual talk, he's scared stiff.'

'Oh, I don't know – '

'Come on Charles, you know I'm right.'

'Well we're both a bit nervous I suppose. But that's good. You live longer if you are nervous.'

'I don't know how you do it, going up there knowing someone is going to try to shoot you down if you don't shoot them first. I'd go mad if either of you got killed.'

Tears started as she clutched his hand.

'At least I get out of going shooting tomorrow!' laughed Charles, trying to change the subject.

'You don't like hunting, do you? You've always got some excuse when Daddy asks you if you can go.'

'Sorry, I didn't mean to offend anyone.'

'No offence taken.'

'It's just that, well, what with all the shooting that goes on in France....'

'You just want to give it a rest?'

'That's right. Well, perhaps it's a little more than that. I've never really liked killing. I know it's got to be done, but I don't see how people can take pleasure in it. I know other people do and I'm being silly and – '

He stopped as she put her hand over his mouth.

'You're not being silly. You're being you, and it's one of the things I love about you. Don't apologise for not liking killing.'

'Well I don't want to offend your father.'

'Perhaps we can wait a bit before telling him what you feel, but I think he'll understand.'

They walked on in silence for a while before breaking out into the open as the sun slowly made its way down towards the trees on the side of the lake.

'Shall we sit in the summer house and watch the sun set?' Olivia suggested as they reached the small but lavishly furnished brick building with its thatched roof, double oak doors to a veranda and curtained windows almost down to floor level. It even had its own toilet and small kitchen at the rear, which made it a palace compared with Charles' accommodation in France. There were a couple of chairs outside, but Olivia opened the door and led them in out of what was becoming a rather cool evening. The soft couches, drinks cupboard, binoculars, bird recognition books and an oil lamp made it perfect for watching the sun go down and the wildlife come out.

They closed the double doors but opened one of the full height windows a little and settled down on the couch, listening to the twittering of the birds settling down for the night and watching the rabbits appearing from their burrows and nibbling at the grass, ever alert for signs of danger.

'Is it very frightening there?' asked Olivia suddenly getting back to the subject that Charles was trying to avoid. He was silent for a moment.

'You can tell me Charles, I'd really like to know.'

'Yes, it is. Young men from both sides getting mown down just because some elderly idiots in their safe offices can't settle their differences in a civilised manner. I've seen some of those Germans. They are scared too, don't understand why they are there, just like us. They call out to their God, the same as we do to ours. Except that it's supposed to be the same God. It's all a mess, Olivia. A mess.'

'Do you know they won't even let us have parachutes?' he continued. 'They say we might use them to escape from a fight. So if the machine catches fire we have to burn with it or jump out and get killed. If we had parachutes we could get down safely, get another plane and be fighting again the next day. They haven't got a clue.'

He looked at her white face and realised she was trembling.

'Oh I am sorry Olivia. I didn't mean to distress you. It'll all be over soon, then we can get back to a normal life. We can get married, have children, do all the things that I dream about in France. And remember I'd far rather be up there in my aeroplane than stuck in those filthy wet trenches jumping out facing bayonets and machine guns.'

17

'I hate being here, unable to help,' she said, her voice shaking and her eyes wet.

He put his arms round her shoulders and drew her to him, but she slipped down out of his grasp and lay with her head on his lap, holding his hand at her neck. He smoothed her hair with his other hand, and felt the softness of her cheek with the back of his fingers.

'Grin, lad,' she said.

He thought for a moment.

'Darling.'

They both loved playing with words, anagrams in particular.

He looked at the setting sun.

'Red east,' he said.

'Dearest, that's west!'

'I know, but 'red stew' doesn't sound so romantic.'

She giggled.

'Lake, move' she said softly, taking his other hand and slowly pulling it down over one of her breasts, under her blouse, until he could feel the hardness of her nipple.

'We shouldn't be doing this,' he said, his voice a little hoarse. 'Anyway that's a spoonerism.'

'It's also an anagram. Do it for me,' she whispered. 'Please.'

'I do love you.'

Neither of them noticed the sun accelerating before it finally disappeared behind the trees.

4

Gordon

'You're very quiet today Don,' said Gordon, stroking his greying well-trimmed beard.

Donald looked up to see his friend's eyes looking at him over his lunchtime beer. Funny how sometimes beards make people look older, sometimes younger. In Gordon's case the grey hairs were a bit of a give-away, showing that he was at least approaching retirement, even though his body showed no trace of gathering fat nor were there many signs of wrinkles on his face.

An old colleague who was working part time prior to retiring altogether, Gordon had got used to his friend's variable moods and knew only too well what the problem probably was, but he seemed particularly down at the moment. They made a point of meeting once a week over a sandwich and a beer for lunch. Susan always complained about the smell of beer when he returned but if it wasn't that it would be something else.

'Just Susan again. She wants to organise me all the time.'

'Perhaps you need organising. Anyway, why not let her? Saves you the bother of deciding what to do.'

'That's not the point.'

'What is the point?'

Donald thought for a moment.

'Well, for instance, the other day she wanted me to go to Warley Place with her, just because her friend told her to go.'

'What's wrong with that? Have you ever been to Warley Place?'

'No. I've heard of it and I know you go there, but don't really know anything about it.'

'Have you heard of Ellen Willmott?'

'Is she that new secretary you were telling me about?'

Gordon groaned.

'Ellen Willmott was a renowned botanist. Her father bought Warley Place in 1875. Remember Warley? Just outside Brentwood, five minutes from here?'

'All right, no need to be sarcastic, of course I know where Warley is. In fact I know where Warley Place is too. It's just that, like I just said, I've never been in.'

'Well she got rare plants from all over the world and got them to grow there. One type of fern needed special conditions so she built a cave for it with a glass roof and a stream running through it. There were doors at each end so that the humidity and temperature were right. That sort of thing.'

'I'm not really into plants.'

'There's more than just plants there. I just find it fascinating, but if you're not interested then – '

'No,' broke in Donald hastily, 'I am. Where did she get the money from?'

'Oh, from money invested by her father and left to her in her mother's will, but also from a very wealthy god-mother. Anyway, the alpine garden was renowned throughout the country – she even got a specialist in from Switzerland to look after it. The rest of the garden was spectacular too. But her money ran out!'

'Shame, but what's that got to do with me?'

'Well the garden got neglected rather and when she died the estate was sold to a local man who wanted to develop it. The rare plants were mostly taken by the beneficiaries and those that were left were sold or stolen. The council refused planning permission so the developer couldn't go ahead with his plans. The big house was demolished, I don't know why, then the Second World War started and the gardens reverted to what was more or less jungle. So in a few years all her work was as if it had never happened.'

'Interesting, if a little sad, but as I said, what's it got to do with me?'

'Ah! The Essex Wildlife Trust look after it now and a group of volunteers, including me, are maintaining it as a nature reserve and at the same time uncovering much of Ellen Willmott's work. So people can walk round – if they are in the Trust – and see the remains of the old cold frames, the alpine gardens, some of the ruins and a number of her original trees. Oh yes, and the walled garden. It takes a lot of work though – you'd be surprised how quickly the nettles and bracken grow, not to mention the sycamore trees! There are also a number of brick features to be restored – the walls of the walled garden, and the terrace to name just a couple. The ha-ha wall has already been renovated.'

'The what?'

'It's a special wall that you couldn't see from the house but kept the deer out.'

'How did it do that?'

'See, there are some interesting things there, especially for an engineer. Someone found that if you dug a ditch with one side sloping grass and the other a vertical brick wall, with the wall on the side nearer the house, the deer couldn't jump over it because they don't like jumping from a downward slope. That way the wall was hidden from the house too.'

'OK, so it is a bit interesting, but I still say what has it got to do with me? I know what you are going to say and the answer is no. I don't know anything about plants and I've never laid a brick in my life.'

'But that's the beauty of it. You learn. And the people there are fantastic to be with. I've only been a few times myself, but I'm absolutely sure it's just what you need. Just come with me once, next Monday, and if you don't like it I won't mention it again.'

'I'll think about it.'

'Well while you do, just remember that it will be half a day – or more if you want – of time on your own or with people you'll like. Time away from Susan.'

'I'll think about it,' Donald repeated.

'You won't,' said Gordon good-naturedly. 'Where are you going for your holiday this year?'

'I suppose it must be irritating hearing about my problems,' said Donald. 'There's nothing worse than other people's problems. I know you'll think I'm silly, but I'll say it anyway. I really admire you. The way you run your life. Sailing over problems.'

'Shut up, can't you? I'm trying to change the subject.'

'Oh yes. Sorry. I'm not sure. She wants to go to Spain again, but after my stomach trouble last year I'd rather stay in this country. And the sun's much too hot.'

'Have you been to Scotland? It's superb. We go every other year. Glasgow's a great place to stay. You've got the shops, theatres, cinemas, and all the mountains and lakes you could want. If you don't mind driving you could go up the west coast and stay in the Highlands for a few days.'

'It's rather a long way to Scotland, isn't it?'

'It doesn't take long up the motorway,' said Gordon, 'Anyway, you can fly or go by train. But if you think it's too far what about the Lake District? Or Yorkshire, that's even closer.'

'Scotland actually sounds quite good,' said Donald warming to the idea. 'I'll talk to Susan about it.'

'Another pint?'

'I'd better not...' begain Donald, but Gordon was already halfway to the bar.

'Be decisive' he said to Don when he returned. 'She'll respect you for it. And lay off those Rennie's, you're eating them like sweets.'

'They're for the indigestion,' he said vacantly, going over in his mind all that Gordon had said.

The more he thought about it, the more he liked the idea. She could do shopping some of the time if the weather was dull, that would keep her happy, or they could walk round the lochs, or even up the mountains if it was fine. Hopefully a bit of both. It could be the making of them. Scotland would probably be best. They could see the Lakes on the way perhaps.

'Well, enough of me,' he continued. 'What have you been up to since last week? Apart from going to Warley Place, that is.'

He half listened while Gordon told him what was going on in the office. Be decisive. Yes, that was the key. Just organise something and tell her. Gordon was right. That had been the problem with her father, being too submissive and not making any decisions and losing respect because of it.

'Scotland?' she'd say. 'I never thought of that. It's supposed to be beautiful. It'll make a change from all that travelling just to get baked and covered in sand...'

Perhaps he would at least drop in at the travel agent's and get a brochure.

5

An Horrific Duel in the Sky

'September and this beastly war is still going strong,' said Harry Henderson. 'Surely it can't last much longer. I just want to get home and get on with my life.'

'Me too,' agreed Charles. 'I've got nothing against the French, but I'll be glad if I never see their country again.'

They sat there in the mess hut looking through the window at the fine drizzle and the desolate-looking airfield with its biplanes in tidy lines on the wet grass – just waiting to be shot up by a marauding Fokker, Harry had said many times.

'I hate killing,' said Charles eventually. 'I know they are the enemy and I know we have to do it, but I still don't like it. I bet most of them have sweethearts or families just the same as us.'

'Yes, but if you don't get them before they get you you're dead. And just think about what it must be like for those poor devils in the trenches. Seeing the man as you kill him. Sticking a bayonet in him perhaps. Christ, how do they do it?'

'I know. What's it all about too? Millions of people getting killed, God knows how much money literally going up in smoke – for what? Because a few megalomaniacs – on both sides – can't get together and sort their problems out. Their problems, not ours. Meanwhile poor old Darwin would be turning in his grave. It's evolution in reverse – the survival of the weakest, all those young enough and healthy enough to fight are marched off to be killed. If every time we flew we had a politician in the back seat I bet the war would be a lot shorter – they might change their minds about not having parachutes, too!'

'Well I suppose they know what they're doing,' said Harry. Then, changing the subject, 'Is that why you always wriggle out of going hunting with us back home? Because you don't like killing?'

'Yes, I suppose it is. Funny, Olivia asked me the same thing.'

'But they are just animals, and they have to be controlled.'

'I know, but it's the idea of enjoying destroying something beautiful that I don't like. If other people want to, that's fine. But

I can't. If I went I'd shoot to miss and then everyone would laugh at me and say I was a rotten shot. I wouldn't like that either and it would embarrass Olivia and your father.'

'You really think very deeply about things, don't you Charles?'

'Maybe. As soon as this affair is over I want to get married Harry. Olivia wanted to do it before, but I didn't want her to be a war widow if the worst happens.'

'We're indestructible old boy,' said Harry with a rather forced laugh. He looked at his watch. 'Time to see Bertie. I wonder what he wants.'

Bertie was the Squadron-Commander and they both had a pretty good idea what he wanted. Something was afoot and they were both to be involved. Charles felt his stomach turning. It was too near the end of the war to get killed now – but pilots were getting killed every day, why not him?

Bertie's office was actually only a partitioned-off area at the end of the hut and they slowly got to their feet and walked the few yards to his door.

'Come in,' came the gruff voice in response to their knock. Anyone hearing him would have expected to see someone in his forties, maybe fifty, not the young man in his mid-twenties – but a tired look on his face that showed he had a lot more than a normal twenty-five year old's worries on his mind.

'Sit down chaps,' he said, putting his papers down and looking at them. That was one of the many things Charles liked about Bertie. Others had to show how busy they were and carried on reading for a minute or picked up the blower. Not him. His men mattered to him.

'Right Captain Henderson, Captain Everington,' he said.

A broad grin spread across Charles' face.

'You are supposed to correct me and say "I'm still a Lieutenant" Charles.'

'Sorry sir. But I'm only a Lieutenant.'

'Not any more you're not. Get the tailor to add the pip asap.'

'Thank you sir. Thank you very much.'

'You've earned it.'

'Well done old boy,' said Harry, shaking his hand. 'Right, we'll be off now then.'

24

'Oh no you don't. There's a big push on this afternoon, you know that. Our kites are committed to help.'

'Yes sir, but we've been told we're not in on it.'

'Correct. Because while the Hun is concentrating on the big one, you two will be sneaking in for a little recce. You'll be flying your Camel Charles, providing cover for Harry in an R.E.8. Pick who you want for your observer Harry.'

'Broadbent will do fine sir, we get on well. Did you say an R.E.8?'

'I did, but if you'd rather use your old F.E.2...'

'No, thank you sir, but I'd prefer to have a Bristol Fighter if there is one available.'

'Sorry, there isn't. You shouldn't meet any Hun, so you should be fine, especially with Charles providing cover. Take off at 1530 hours, thirty minutes after the rest have gone, that will give the enemy time to get after them and not you. Right, here's where you are going...'

He got up and pointed to a circle drawn on the map pinned to his wall.

'... There are reports of a build up of vehicles there, but we don't know how many or what sort of vehicles. Don't hang about. Just one pass over the target, take your pictures and get out. Understood?'

'Yes sir.'

'Right. Here's your maps. Don't forget, one pass. Don't take any chances, especially at this stage of the war. Good luck.'

'Thank you sir,' they said in unison, saluting before turning to leave.

'See? Should be easy,' said Harry once outside. 'Trouble for the others, milk run for us.'

'No such thing as easy in this war,' said Charles soberly. 'Anyway, what's with the Harry Tate? You might as well have stayed with the B.E.2.'

'What's got into you? You've gone up before knowing the odds are against you and not worried. Now the opposition are going to be otherwise engaged you're down in the dumps. The Harry Tate is replacing the B.E.2, you know it is. It's a step up. Yes, the Bristol would have been better, but you have to be thankful for small mercies.'

25

'I know, but it seems so bloody unfair. For the first time I'm thinking about the future. The war's nearly over and I want to settle down with Livie. Have a family. Do the ordinary things. Enjoy life.'

'Well don't get too cautious. Careful yes, but cautious no. You get yourself killed that way. Come on, let's have a bite to eat then take another look at those maps and work out a game plan.'

'No food for me Harry, it makes me sleepy and sleepy is the last thing I want to be this afternoon. As far as the plan is concerned I'll fly on your starboard side and above. That way they'll go for me first and I'll be free to turn – you know how quick the Camel goes that way.'

Harry yawned and grinned. He knew very well how quickly the Camel rolled to the right and how quickly it could turn through a full circle and get behind its attacker. With its rotary engine and low rolling inertia it really was manoeuvrable, but its nose dropped when turning that way and without a lot of rudder it could flick into a spin. It had killed a lot of careless or inexperienced pilots without a shot being fired. Once behind its opponent though the twin Vickers machine guns were lethal. Charles flew it as though it was part of him and if he couldn't win a dogfight no-one could. Charles was disappointed Harry was only getting the R.E.8 though. The F.E 2 was fine in its day, but was a bit past it now, although plenty were still in use. Lacking in speed, manoeuvrability and defensive armament Harry was lucky to be able to leave it on the ground. The trouble was, the R.E.8, or Harry Tate as it was nick-named after the comedian, was also rather slow, struggled for altitude and was not particularly manoeuvrable, so was only marginally better than Harry's previous mount. As Bertie had said, this should be an uneventful operation though so all should be well.

Charles continued. 'We'll fly at ten thousand – I don't think the Tate will get much past that. We fly past the target, go down low and come in fast from the rear where they won't be expecting us. As the man said, one run only then out.'

'OK. I'll lead, Broadbent is pretty good at finding the way.'

'Fine.'

'Anything you need sir?'

They both looked up as their batman stood over them.

'Sandwiches for the flight?'

26

'Just one thing,' said Charles nonchalantly, stripping his jacket off. 'Get another pip sewn on, will you?'

Smithy grinned from ear to ear.

'Certainly sir.'

'Damn,' said Charles as Smithy disappeared. 'My other jacket is being cleaned. Got oil over it.'

'No problem,' said Harry. 'Just have your thick pullover on under your flying jacket. I've done it before.'

Grabbing the rest of their flying gear they made their way to their aircraft to check them out, Harry joined by Broadbent from the Sergeants' Mess. They were both very particular about the pre-flight checks. Some didn't bother, but a chafed wire or a loose screw could cost them their lives.

Half an hour later Charles was bouncing down the grass strip, his Clerget engine roaring away in front of him. Easing back on the stick suddenly he and his aircraft were transformed. It might be called a camel – a nickname rather than an official one, brought about by the humped fairing over the breeches of the two Vickers machine guns in front of the cockpit – but it certainly didn't act like one. Tricky to fly until you got used to it, but when you did it was a lethal fighting machine.

He banked and turned to follow Harry as they headed towards the front line, struggling for height. It was less common to be fired at by your own side when you were going than when coming back but it had happened, so the higher the better.

Ten minutes later he was looking down at the trenches, snaking as far as the eye could see in both directions. God it must be awful down there, unable to dodge the shells as they came in, then having to climb out and walk into the withering fire from the enemy machine guns. Charles didn't think he could have done it. It might be dangerous up here, but at least you could pit your skill against someone else's, not just rely on luck.

He started screwing his head round and looking up. The sun was breaking through the murky sky which would help their navigation and photographs, but also made them easier to be seen by the Hun. Don't lose sight of Harry though, he thought as he weaved to uncover the blind spots. He gave his goggles a wipe with a cloth, but the hot castor oil soon covered them again. The windscreen was at best translucent by now. That was the trouble with rotary engines – the unburnt castor oil mixing with the

27

exhaust gases ended up over the pilot. Just when you really needed to see properly your goggles were covered in the stuff. It was the only oil that wasn't dissolved by petrol and while they were on duty all the pilots stank of it.

Half an hour later, shifting uncomfortably in his basket-work seat, he saw Broadbent waving to him and pointing down. He leaned out into the slipstream and saw their objective – lines of vehicles, too small to be identified from up here.

As planned they carried on past as if it was no concern of theirs until with the vehicles out of sight they turned, still at ten thousand feet, and dived to build up a bit of speed before overflying at one thousand feet. Charles felt the aircraft shaking and the wind howling through the struts of his biplane built up to a crescendo before he levelled out.

Broadbent in the back seat of the R.E.8 would normally have kept an eye on the rear but Charles saw that he was busy readying his camera, so twisted his head round to make sure all was well. That was when he saw the dots coming from the sun. He dived ahead of Harry and waggled his wings to let him know of trouble, then pointed back. Broadbent was at his guns in the back now, the camera set aside for the moment. Good man, thought Charles. No point in heroics getting perfect pictures if they were in a burning wreck in a French field.

He banked and turned to face the attackers. God, there must be a dozen of them, Albatrosses, they looked like. He charged at them, guns blazing, and they broke in all directions. He banked to the right, nose dropped a bit, damn, there was one. His guns chattered again and he saw holes appearing in the engine cowling and the aircraft dived away with smoke pouring from the nose. Turn, bank, dive, he twisted and turned with aircraft everywhere. Suddenly holes appeared in his wing and he felt a hammer blow in his leg. Fear took over and he automatically broke right again, but not able to use his right leg properly made control difficult. He was streaming with sweat and oil covered his windscreen and goggles. He knew he wasn't going to make it back this time. A biplane came into his vision as he turned and he fired more with hope than expectation, the instinct for survival keeping him going. He just had time to gasp in horror as he saw the pilot's head disintegrate, flesh and blood whipped back in the slipstream, before again trying to turn out of trouble as bullets thumped through the canvas wings into his own aircraft.

His nose dipped but he somehow managed to get the aircraft banking round for a further very quick three-sixty turn and was once more behind one of his attackers. A long burst sent this second Albatros down. Then his engine faltered as more bullets poured into it from yet another enemy aircraft. Fabric was peeling off his wings and a bracing wire trailed behind in the wind. It wouldn't be long now. Please, no fire, he begged, not with the petrol tank right behind him. He tried to break to the right again but his leg gave way and the plane flicked into a spin. He was too low to recover but tried anyway. He just had time to see Harry's machine dive into the ground and explode before his own plane ploughed its way across a field towards some trees.

The next thing he remembered was a German pilot pulling him out of the cockpit. He saw his wrecked Camel standing there, smoke starting to appear from the engine, and the burning remains of the R.E.8 beyond. The German dragged him away as flames appeared in the smoke.

His rescuer had just got him clear and laid him down on the grass when with a whoofing noise the petrol tank blew up. A huge fireball engulfed his plane.

'You are very lucky man,' said his rescuer in a guttural but not unkind voice. 'Your aircraft is no more.'

'Thank you,' said Charles automatically with his eyes not on his own burning wreckage but that of Harry's. He forced himself to his feet, staggered a couple of steps towards the flames and saw the ground coming up to meet him before blackness took him into its comforting arms.

6

Ellen Willmott confides in Jacob Maurer

'Who is there? I have a pistol!' came a rather high pitched voice from the darkness.

'Sorry Miss Ellen,' said Jacob Maurer, 'It's Jacob. I'll be on my way then.'

'No, stay a while if you will Jacob. Sit here with me.'

He made out her figure then, sitting next to her telescope, motioning to a garden seat. Wishing now that he had not ventured out this evening, he did as she bade him.

'Are you not well Jacob?' Her voice was much softer, but retained the authority that came so naturally to her. She was in his opinion the greatest woman gardener that ever lived, certainly in England and possibly in the world. Some thought that title should be applied to her friend Gertrude Jekyll, most probably thought they were equals, but for Jacob there was no contest. His own knowledge of alpine plants may well have approached or even exceeded hers – which was why she employed him here at Warley Place – but her grasp of botany as a whole was awesome. And still she had time to gaze at the stars!

'Quite well, Miss Ellen. I could not rest and thought that a walk would do me good. It is so peaceful out here at night.' He fiddled nervously with his big moustache.

'I would have thought you'd have had enough of it, working here all day. Do be careful of the tripwires though, I do not want to have to set them again.'

With so much time and effort put into developing her hybrid daffodils she was sure someone would come into the garden at night and make off with some. She had employed a security man once but when making her late evening round had found him asleep. She sacked him and set up a system of tripwires that set off air guns and rang bells to frighten such intruders away or at least give her time to go after them with her gun. There was something incongruous about someone like Ellen Willmott with a gun, but he wouldn't like to have to face her with it.

'I suppose you miss Rosina very much?'

'Indeed I do. Working during the day keeps my mind off the gap she has left, but the nights are difficult. Coming out here calms my troubled mind.'

Rosina, his wife, had borne him nine children but had just recently died of tuberculosis. He felt a lump appear in his throat as he thought of her. He'd been relieved at first when she finally passed on. The continual gasping for breath, hardly eased by the bloody sputum that she brought up each morning, the pain in her chest that she bore so well and the wasting away of her body so that she looked almost skeletal, all that was at an end. Her suffering was no more, he had told himself. Death was a merciful release. But now he just felt guilty. Why should she have had to go through this? What sort of god would visit that sort of torture on his subjects? The future looked so bleak, so empty. He would have gone mad without his garden in Warley Place. What a pity she hadn't lived to take advantage of the little house and pension he had been promised when he retired.

'Do you wish you had never come here? Do you wish you had stayed in Geneva with Henri Correvon?'

'Oh no, Miss Ellen. I would never have had the chance to work with you and to help you to develop the alpine garden.'

'I could never have done it without you Jacob. But now, your children, it must be difficult for you.'

'My cousin, Friedi, helps with them. But yes, it is difficult.'

'You've been here, what, twenty-five years Jacob?'

'Yes, twenty-five years, since 1894, seeing the alpine garden grow to its magnificent best. It has been difficult though, since the war started, keeping it in shape and looking after so many other things since Mr Preece and then Mr Fielder moved on.'

Why Mr Preece had been removed from his post as Head Gardener was a mystery to Jacob, but it was obvious to most of the staff that Miss Willmott was in some financial difficulty and that if she couldn't afford him then she couldn't afford Fielder either. Now Jacob was trying to cover for them as well as continuing to keep the alpine garden up to scratch. It was an impossible task to look after fifty-five acres of garden, even if much of it was meadow or lawn, but Miss Willmott was a hard taskmaster and would not accept excuses. She said she would take over from Fielder, but she was away so often and interfered so much with what he was trying to do, she just made it worse. He hoped that now the war was over her finances would improve and she could get some more help.

'Ah yes, poor Mr Preece,' she said sadly. 'Did you know he died last year of influenza? It's been sweeping the country. You would think that by now they would have found a way to stop it killing so many. Even more than the war itself, they say. I think we are safe now, especially here, but I wouldn't venture into town too often Jacob.'

'But the children need to go to school.'

'Yes.'

They sat there in silence for a bit, Ellen Willmott apparently at ease, Jacob feeling distinctly uncomfortable. This was most uncharacteristic of his employer. She could be friendly at times, yes, but not like this.

'Do you look at the stars, Jacob?'

'Sometimes, Miss Ellen. Don't know much about them though.'

'Well this is a good night for it, with no moon and a clear sky. See that one, that bright one there?'

'Yes, it is bright indeed.'

'That is Jupiter. It's a planet, and it has nine moons. It would need a bigger telescope than mine to see them all, but I can see four of them with my own instrument.'

'Is Jupiter the nearest planet to us then? Not Mars?'

'No, not the nearest, but it is the biggest. Mars and Venus are nearer but very much smaller, although Venus too can appear very bright. Jupiter is the next planet out from Mars, with a belt of asteroids between them.'

'Asteroids?'

'Space rubble. Some of them are very big, many miles across, but most are quite small. Even the big ones are very small compared with the Earth though.'

'I wonder if there are people there looking at us, wondering how we get by with only one moon. It must be quite a sight, having nine.'

'They would have to be very different from us Jacob, it's very cold indeed out there so far from the sun and any persons on it would quickly sink beneath the surface, it is of such light substance.'

32

She was a strange woman indeed, he thought. So different from any others that he had known. Not that he had known many, apart from his Rosina and his cousin Friedi. She knew so much about plants and gardening and that would have been astonishing enough. But she knew about stars and planets, her music brought tears to his eyes sometimes as he heard it through the open windows in the summer, her photographs and her paintings were something to behold. Was there nothing she could not do? Perhaps that was why she had never experienced true love – no man would dare try to live up to her standards and would know pretty soon what she felt of him when he failed!

He gazed at the sky and wondered how many stars there were. There must be thousands of them, some so bright they seemed to be on fire, others he could only just see.

'There is a sort of cloud across the sky,' he said. 'There are more stars there. It looks like a trail of spilt milk through the heavens.'

'That is the Milky Way Jacob. It is the galaxy in which our own star belongs and it is shaped like a sort of disc. If you look along the disk there are more stars and it looks like that. If you look out from the disc there are not so many.'

'I had always imagined it as a dandelion gone to seed. But you say it looks more like a crocus meadow in spring. Look along it from an angle and it looks purple all over. But look at it from above and the grass between them becomes clear.'

'Yes Jacob, that is the idea. But we speak of our own galaxy alone. You may be right that the universe does look like a dandelion gone to seed, for there are many galaxies and each galaxy may be a seed. Each of those seeds is like a Milky Way, except that there are many more than there are seeds on a dandelion head. Some of those stars you can see are in fact galaxies like ours, each one composed of many thousands of stars.'

'They must be a very long way away.'

'They certainly are. So far that neither you nor I could visualise it.'

'It is beautiful Miss Ellen. I can see why you come out here sometimes at night. Not as beautiful to me as the alpine garden in full colour, but beautiful. A little frightening too. It makes me feel very small.'

They both sat there looking. Ellen Willmott finally broke the silence.

'Things are difficult financially Jacob, but I will try to get you some help. We must not let the alpine garden go, nor the walled garden. Nor anything else if we can help it, but I fear we are too understaffed to cope with it all.'

Jacob said nothing. All this was known to him, but for his employer to admit it was unheard of.

'Is there anything in particular you feel needs attention?'

'The walls of the walled garden are in need of repair, particularly the south wall.'

'Mind the *Berberis fremontii*.'

'Oh yes, Miss Ellen, those spines can be vicious.'

'Jacob!'

'Yes Miss Ellen, we will make sure we don't damage the *Berberis fremontii*. Or the *Cytisus virgatus* or the *Elaeagnus argenteus* or anything else growing along that wall.'

'Well I sometimes get the impression that you care less about the walled garden than your alpines.'

'That may be true,' said Jacob. 'After all you brought me here for the alpine garden and its upkeep is enough for any man. You have spent a fortune on it, so it would be a great pity for it to be allowed to suffer now. We can just about keep up with the weeds in there, watering the plants and keeping the ferns moist in their cave. The walled garden too we can probably cope with, but elsewhere I fear we will struggle a little. Even the cold frames are suffering, as are the greenhouses, and watering everything outside those areas is beyond us.'

Ellen Willmott did not argue. Jacob Maurer knew that he was essential to the upkeep of the alpine garden. There were others who could look after the walled garden though, and she was aware of that.

'I may be able to help with an assistant. If all goes well I will see you tomorrow and he can see to the wall.'

'But can we afford it?'

'I will see you tomorrow.'

He had been dismissed.

7

Susan

'Scotland? You've booked a holiday in Scotland? Why on earth would we want to go to Scotland?'

'Well the scenery is fantastic, and the shops in Glasgow and Edinburgh are really good. Anyway, it would be a change.'

'The weather is awful. At least in Spain you can guarantee sunshine. We always go there, with Mum.'

'We could do both. Go to Spain with your mother and have a week in Scotland.'

'We can't afford both. Where did this idea come from? Gordon?'

The furrow between his eyebrows deepened.

'I'm thinking about going to Warley Place,' he said. 'They need volunteers to work on restoring the brickwork and seeing to the trees and plants – some of them are very rare.'

'Gordon put you up to that too, didn't he? When I suggested going you objected, probably because it was Doreen's idea, but when Gordon suggests it you can't get there fast enough.'

'No,' protested Donald. 'I did ask him about it, but it was my idea to go. As I said, I thought about what you said and wanted to learn something practical that might help in our own garden and that's the place to do it.'

She knew he was still lying but she couldn't argue with his motive.

'Do you know about Warley Place?' he asked, trying to get out of the confrontation they were now in.

'Of course I do. Ellen Willmott's old place.'

'Oh. I didn't really know anything about it until Gordon told me.'

'Is this the same Gordon that didn't put you up to it?'

'Ah. Yes.'

Her face relaxed slightly. He really was impossible sometimes but when he put that boyish contrite expression on his face she always felt sorry for him.

'Well don't come back with any bad habits from that lot.'

35

'But they are all professional people,' he protested. 'Retired, like me. There's a doctor, a surveyor, an engineer, all professional people who want to do something interesting and useful.'

'It must be tedious for you stuck in here all day,' he continued. 'You could always come too, if you wanted,' regretting his words as soon as they were out.

'And restore brickwork? No thank you.'

'I'll get on with the shed then.'

Susan glanced at the clock as the doorbell rang; eleven on the dot. She went down the hall from the kitchen and opened the door.

'Hello mother,' she said. 'Come on in. The coffee's on; I thought we'd have it in the garden today, it's too good to stay inside.'

'As you wish dear.' She looked in to the lounge as they passed the door. 'Donald not reading then?'

'No, the weather is too good to be indoors so he's busy in the garden.'

'He doesn't know the first thing about flowers.'

'No, I've got him tidying the shed and painting that weatherproofing stuff on before it rains again. Then he'll be turning the compost. And there's some rubbish to take to the tip.'

'Oh well, as long as he's busy.'

They sat down at the little round plastic table with the umbrella on top to shade them from the sun.

'You know Donald's going through a difficult time at the moment mother. Retirement isn't easy on a man. It's a bit of a shock after going to work regularly for forty years and then suddenly it's all over.'

'Difficult for you too, having a man under your feet all the time. Some men need a woman to keep them up to scratch, otherwise they'd just sit about all day. The lawn could do with cutting.'

Susan started pouring the coffee out.

'There's some clover there too, I see. And isn't that a dandelion?'

'Probably mother, but I don't really mind things like that growing on the lawn, as long as they don't get out of hand; and we like to keep the grass just a little bit long when it's as hot and dry as this.'

Donald emerged from the shed, dust clinging to his clothes.

'Good morning,' he said, just a little warily. 'Lovely day.'

He had a slight smile on his face. One that said to Susan '…for sitting watching someone else work.'

'I'll just paint that wood treatment on the shed dear. It shouldn't smell too much.'

'Just don't get any on the flowers, it kills them,' said Susan's mother.

'Actually this stuff doesn't,' said Donald. 'Not unless you pour it over them I suppose.'

'Mum,' said Susan as Donald wandered back to the shed. 'Don's trying hard to help me and I'm trying to help him. You are right, it is difficult for both of us.'

Susan lapsed into silence. With her father dying soon after his own retirement they did see rather a lot of her mother. Donald didn't complain but Susan had to admit to herself that she could be a bit critical at times. Not just of Donald, of all men. She hadn't had an easy time with her own husband though, always having to organise things for him and Donald was similar in some ways.

'The aquilegias are looking nice, aren't they Mum.'

'Yes dear, very nice.'

'No, they are dieramas. But they are looking good too. The aquilegias are over there.'

Donald would be horrified if he knew he and her mother had something in common. Neither could remember the names of plants. The only difference was that Donald admitted it.

'I know, I know. I was looking at the dieramas too. I think Donald has missed a bit on the shed. Will you tell him?'

'No mother, not yet. He'll spot it in a minute.'

Funny really, how she criticised Donald no end to his face, but if anyone else did it, even her own mother, she defended him. Well, most of the time anyway.

'What's happening about our holiday? You'll be coming with us to Spain again I hope?'

'I'm not sure mother. Donald was talking about going to Scotland.'

'What? You're not going of course.'

'I don't know. When he told me I said no, but we haven't spoken about it since.'

'As long as he's got the message.'

'He's been talking about going to Warley Place to help there.'

'With all that needs doing here? What's Warley Place?'

'A nature reserve at Warley. Actually I thought it might do us both good if he went. He needs to have another interest and this one won't cost anything.'

'Tell him he can go when the lounge is decorated, the shed and fences weatherproofed and now I come to look the outside of the house could do with some paint before winter arrives.'

'No, I don't think I'll stop him. I do get ratty and it might partly be that he's under my feet all the time. There I am cooking and ironing and he's sitting there reading.'

'Ah, cooking and ironing. Why can't he – '

'No mother. Decorating, putting shelves up, cutting the grass, doing the compost, fine. Cooking and ironing, no.'

'I don't see why not. Other men do.'

'Other men do lots of things I would prefer Donald didn't.'

'All right then, if he goes to Warley what are you going to do?'

'What do you mean?'

'If that's going to be his interest, what's yours going to be?'

'I have my garden.'

'But outside your garden? You need a bit of excitement.'

'I'll think about it. Perhaps sign up for one of those adult education classes.'

'I said excitement. Pity you don't drive, then we could go and visit some gardens.'

'I suppose. Donald's has always had the car for work and when we go anywhere we go together, so I never really got round to learning.'

They sat in silence for a while.

'Right, I must go now dear. I told Gladys I'd pop in to see her.'

'OK mother. See you tomorrow probably.'

She saw her mother to the door, waved goodbye, and sat at the table outside for a few minutes. Perhaps that was indeed what she needed. Another interest would help their relationship; stop her getting so scratchy with Donald. Something like Warley Place for

Donald too would probably help him deal with his retirement better.

She picked up The Independent, glanced at the unfinished crossword and then put it down again. She just wasn't in the mood for it this morning. Perhaps she had been a bit hard on him about Scotland. He had a point, they should get away on their own and they could actually manage both, for one year at least.

8

Ellen Willmott is Inclined to Help

'Dr Townsend,' said Robinson.

Ellen Willmott finished dead-heading and rose to her feet, taking her leather gardening gloves off and dropping them to the ground.

'Good to see you again Ellen,' said the doctor, extending his hand. She shook it warmly.

'And you, Stephen.'

The psychiatrist was one of the few men who made a real impression on her. His upright bearing, the black hair turning white at the temples, the eyes that met hers, the quiet confidence that he exuded and the common sense advice he gave, all indicated a true professional; someone who really did know what he was about, unlike some of the charlatans that she had met.

'I spoke to you about placing one of my patients here,' he said, getting straight to the point.

'Ah, yes. I have given the matter a lot of thought. Having someone here who is a little unstable, well, it's quite a responsibility. Not just for me, but for Jacob and the others too.'

'He's not unstable. He's just lost his memory and is a bit confused at times. Who wouldn't be in his situation?'

'I don't know. Some of my plants are irreplaceable.'

'Please, Ellie?' begged Dr Townsend. 'He's a young man who's done his bit for his country, lost his memory and gets a bit jittery at sudden noises, that's all. I really don't want to put him in the asylum with the rest. He's obviously well educated, musical and artistic – this would be just the place for him.'

Ellen Willmott shuddered. The thought of any gentleman going into the asylum as a result of doing his duty in that awful war horrified her. She also owed Stephen Townsend a lot for giving her assistance with some of her gardeners when they came back from France, otherwise he wouldn't have got past her front gate. She could really do without the hassle; she had enough worries of her own at the moment, but on the other hand free labour, with just his food to be found, might be useful.

40

'You say you don't want to put him in the asylum. Isn't that where he is now?'

'Well, actually he is staying in my house at the moment, but he is bored to tears. He needs to work and to mix with other people.'

Yes, she thought. Typical Stephen Townsend. He wasn't asking her to do anything he hadn't done himself.

'Are you sure he's not violent or destructive? If he ended up killing my plants...'

'Definitely not. He loves beauty. That's part of his problem; he hated the destruction, the ugliness of war.'

'Does he know anything about gardening?'

'I don't know, but I do know he is meticulous in all he does and is a quick learner.'

'Very well Stephen,' she sighed finally. 'What is his name?'

'Er... Alexander.'

'What do you mean "Er Alexander?" Are you not sure?'

'As I said, he can't remember anything. Temporarily we hope. He got captured near the end of the war and was being looked after by the Germans. He had a bullet wound and some other injuries but the main problem was that he seemed to have lost his memory. He didn't have any identification so they called him Mr X. Alexander sounded better so our nurses called him that. We don't know anything else but I'm sure working here will be of great help to him. And I hope to you.'

'Did he not have any papers with him?'

'Only a photograph of him with a beautiful young lady. None of us could recognise the background, it could be anywhere. He just freezes up when he looks at it but won't part with it. One day perhaps it will trigger something.'

'I hope I'm not going to regret this, because if I do so then will you. When will he be here?'

'Actually he's in my car.' He did have the grace to look a bit sheepish.

'You take a lot for granted!'

'No, I don't think so. You don't suffer fools gladly, but you have a soft spot for those in genuine trouble. Especially gentlemen or gentlewomen, and he seems to be a gentleman. Shall I bring him over?'

'Very well, bring him over and I'll show him where he'll be working and introduce him to Jacob.'

She started to move, winced and bent down to rub her knees. The rheumatism had been kept at bay enough so that others did not notice, but she dreaded the fate that had struck her mother in later years – being confined to a wheelchair, unable to tend to her beloved plants.

'Are you sure you don't want me to do something about that?' he asked.

'I'm all right,' she said sharply. Then, seeing his car in the distance, 'And so are you, from the look of it.'

'Oh that?' he said, seeing the direction of her gaze. 'It's an Austin Vitesse.'

'I know what it is.' She was still annoyed with herself for letting him see her stiffness. 'Four cylinder, 23 horsepower. Elliptic rear springs I believe. Top speed fifty miles an hour. You got the electric starter and electric lighting of course.'

'Ah, well, actually no.'

She sniffed and turned away, ignoring both the car and the figure in the passenger seat, making her way towards the bridge over the gorge, putting her gloves back on as she walked, while her visitor went to fetch his patient.

'Jacob!' she called, and when he had not answered or come within a few seconds she repeated herself somewhat louder.

'Oh, there you are,' she said as he came scrambling up out of the bottom of the gorge. Did you not hear me the first time?'

'Sorry Miss Ellen,' he said passively, 'I was unblocking the stream and didn't hear at first for the noise of the water.'

Sometimes she really wished he would answer her back; nothing seemed to penetrate that calmness, not when he was working on his alpine garden. She briefly wondered if he knew it annoyed her so did it all the more, but dismissed the idea. Jacob was Jacob – unique and reliable, even with personal problems that would have destroyed many a man.

'Come with me, Jacob.'

Jacob obediently wiped his hands on his apron and followed his mistress towards the house. She said nothing to him as the two men walked to meet them.

'Miss Ellen Willmott, can I introduce you to Alexander?'

She turned to her visitor and looked him straight in the eye. He did not blink or look away, only when it would have been bad manners to continue to stare. He had an honest open look about him and had certainly been well brought up, but there was a haunted look about those eyes. They hid a secret that hurt him, and hurt him badly. Something touched her heart and she smiled at him, pleased to see an answering smile on his lips and in his eyes. On impulse she took off her gardening glove again and reached out a hand, which he shook with a firm but not too strong a grasp.

'Jacob, meet your new assistant,' she said. 'Things have been a bit confused lately, what with the war and one thing and another,' she continued to Alexander. 'I am in charge but Jacob really runs the garden, with somewhat limited resources now. He will show you where you will be staying – in the bothy I think Jacob, for the time being anyway – and then what work you will be doing.'

'Thank you,' said Alexander. 'May I ask what a bothy is?'

'It's a cottage for the staff who couldn't find accommodation in the village,' explained Jacob. 'Or a couple of cottages actually. They used to be overflowing but they are almost empty now. You'll have your own room. It's up on the other side of the road just past the north lodge. I'll show you later.'

'That sounds fine. Thank you very much Miss Willmott.'

Ellen Willmott grunted a non-committal reply and Jacob led him off.

'You are getting sentimental in your old age!' Stephen Townsend commented with a smile.

'No harm in doing someone a good turn,' she retorted, returning to dead-heading. 'Don't we know anything about him at all? What uniform was he wearing? Was he an officer?'

'He was actually wearing some old German work clothes. No-one knows what happened to his uniform, but I'd say he was an officer, wouldn't you?'

She nipped off a flower head that was past its best.

'Are there any papers? Do I have to sign anything?'

'We only have his temporary papers and no, there is nothing for you to sign. When he has recovered, which we hope he will, then we can get him sorted out.'

'You only hope he will get better?'

43

'Well, to be honest, we can't be certain. But if he doesn't get better here he won't get better anywhere. Your supervision, Jacob's calm demeanour and these gardens are just what he needs. Let me know if you need any advice or help.'

He was talking to her back. She was oblivious to him now, back to her plants. He called out his thanks and walked back to his car. When the sound of its engine had died away she straightened up again and looked around. A hundred gardeners hustled and bustled about the garden at one time, now there were just a handful, not one of them in sight, and she was glad of the chance of an unpaid albeit totally inexperienced helper. How had it come to this? She had blamed the war, and certainly it had not helped. Sales of her masterpiece *The Genus Rosa* had been hit badly by the conflict, but that alone would hardly have scratched the surface of what she owed. Tresserve and Boccanegra, her properties in France and Italy, would both have to go but she had invested so much time and money in their purchase and improvement she really didn't want to sell them. Funny how people could push unwelcome thoughts away into distant parts of their brains and shut the doors.

At least the alpine garden was still well kept. Goodness knows how Jacob managed it. She slowly walked down the slope on the stone steps to see what he had been up to today, stopping to pull up the occasional weed or to mark with the little red sticks plants that really urgently needed watering.

The little *Campanula garganica*, no more than three inches high, with its blue white-centred flowers and ivy-like leaves was doing well. The *Campanula raineri*, that was doing well too – but she wondered how long for, it was delicate as well as rare. The deep saucer shaped flowers looked beautiful on short leafy stems.

The murmur of distant voices disturbed her reverie. They were coming back, Jacob and Alex. She saw them through the trees, walking towards the walled garden.

Then she heard the sound of aircraft engines and looked up. Noisy things, but attractive in their way. A little biplane came towards them, quite low. Then another, practicing its war manoeuvres no doubt, dived upon it and turned away at the last minute. She had no idea what sort it was, she was only interested in things she could possess and she had no intention of ever possessing an aeroplane.

44

She glanced back at Jacob and saw Alex cringing against a rock, crouched with his hands over his ears. As the aircraft disappeared over the house Jacob helped him to his feet and put his arm round him, talking to him, reassuring him presumably.

Ellen Willmott quietly continued her walk along the garden, away from the two of them. Alex would not want her to see him crying.

9

Depression

'It was a close thing, I can tell you,' Donald said to Gordon as he sipped his drink. 'But I think it's worked out all right. For a moment I thought the Glasgow idea had blown the whole thing. But it's OK now. At least, Warley is. I think. Not so sure about Scotland. I hope it really is as lovely as you say. I did tell you what she said, didn't I?'

'Yes, you did,' said Gordon hastily. And yes, Scotland is as beautiful as I said it is. It's the snow that really makes it, I think.'

'But we're going in August.'

'That's right.'

'What?'

'I'm joking, I'm joking. Don't panic. It won't snow in August. Might rain a bit, but it won't snow. Almost certainly it won't.'

'Look, stop joking for a minute Gordon, this is serious. Tell me the worst about Glasgow. What's the weather really like?'

'Well, it's like most of the western areas of the UK. The winds generally come from the Atlantic, full of moisture, and they precipitate it when they rise over the hills by the coast.'

'You mean it rains a lot.'

'Well, yes. About twice as much as in the east I believe. About eighty inches a year instead of forty.'

'Oh no! Anything else?'

'Well it's colder than down here of course. But you'd expect that, it's nearer the North Pole. It can be lovely sometimes though. Strolling along by a loch on a hot steamy summer's day, mountains all around. Really romantic. Do you the world of good. Of course the warm weather does bring the midges out.'

'Midges? What midges?'

'Oh, just some nasty vicious little flies that like the taste of human blood. I think you can get something for them though.'

'Oh God I've blown it. I'm dead. She'll murder me. Why didn't I just put up with Spain again?'

'Don, for Christ's sake shut up. Can't you be a man and do what you want to do for a change? OK, I shouldn't keep teasing you.

46

But I can't help it, you just ask for it with all your whinging. You never used to be like that in the office. What on earth has come over you? People come from all over Europe, America, Japan, everywhere to see Scotland. It's beautiful. Yes it might rain, but not enough to spoil a holiday, not in the summer. It might be cooler than here, but so what? I can't stand the heat in the middle of summer, here or in Spain. There might be midges, though I was there for five years and never got bitten, but put some repellent on. Think positive. Enjoy it.'

Don stood there open mouthed at the outburst.

'I suppose you're right,' he said eventually. 'It must be irritating for you. As from now I'll be more positive. But you don't understand what it's like. Does the midge repellent smell at all?'

Gordon groaned.

Donald looked at his watch and quickened his pace. How could he have forgotten about Susan's elder sister Margaret coming to dinner with her husband George when he made the appointment? If he was late she'd skin him alive.

With a sigh of relief he turned up the path to the surgery, opened the door and froze. It was packed. He contemplated turning round and leaving, but saw the receptionist looking. He went over.

'Er...I have an appointment with Dr Shaw, but perhaps I'll come back later.'

She smiled. 'These are all waiting for the other doctors. Dr Shaw will be free in a minute or two. You must be Mr Johnson?'

'Oh. Sorry. That's right.'

'Just sit down, I'll call you when he's ready.'

Self-consciously he went to the only vacant seat there was. Why did everyone look at you when you came in? Feeling guilty that he didn't actually look ill, he put a pained expression on his face and casually let his gaze wander round the room.

The hush had been replaced by the hum of conversation again. He tried not to listen, but random snatches penetrated his defences.

'It's my legs, they've never been the same since...'

'The old trouble, you know, down there...'

'Ooh you don't look well at all...'

Suddenly he wanted to get up and run out. The voices all merged into one cacophony of noise that echoed in his head. He started to get up but his legs felt wobbly and he was worried he

47

would fall over. He started to panic, but suddenly realised someone was calling his name.

'Mr Johnson? Dr Shaw will see you now.'

He smiled a thank you, got to his feet without in fact falling over, and walked nervously in the direction of her wave.

Down a short corridor, to a door marked 'Dr Shaw', half open. He stopped outside, swallowing to clear his throat and rehearse his symptoms, afraid he would miss one.

'Come in, don't be shy.'

He walked in and sat in the proffered chair, while the doctor studied a card with hieroglyphics on it.

'Well what can I do for you? Haven't seen you for a long time. You're one of my more healthy ones.'

'W w well I er not sure um yes I suppose I am healthy really.'

'Take a deep breath and tell me about it.'

'It sounds so silly now.'

'Let me be the judge of that. Tell me. Everything.'

'Well it is a bit confusing. To me, anyway. I've got this lump in my throat. Not all the time, but when it appears I can't swallow and I think I'm going to choke. I can't feel any lumps with my fingers, but I know it's there. My heart starts thumping for no reason, I think I'm going to have a heart attack. Sometimes I can't eat, even though I'm hungry. I just sit and chew it, but I can't swallow. And friends are beginning to laugh at me because of the tablets I take for indigestion. But I have to; I feel sick and keep bringing up wind.'

'Do you sleep well?'

'Not really, not usually. I drop off, but wake up in the middle of the night with everything going round and round in my mind.'

'The sick feeling. Do you actually vomit?'

'No. I wouldn't dare!' He smiled weakly at his own joke, wondering at the thoughtful expression on the doctor's face as he came round and examined Don's hands.

'What about noises?'

'Well I didn't want to mention that as well, but they do sometimes startle me. The telephone makes me jump out of my skin. Must have developed sensitive ears.'

'Troubles at work?'

'I retired recently.'

'Oh. Money worries then?'

'No, we live within our budget.'

The Wall is a story based on life at Warley Place; life in 1919 during Ellen Willmott's reign, and life today when Essex Wildlife Trust volunteers toil to keep it from reverting to the wilderness it became upon its owner's death in 1934. The idea for the plot arose when the author was chipping the old mortar from the wall of the walled garden and some bricks came loose. To find out more you will have to read the book, but suffice it to say that at least one proof-reader found that she was laughing out loud one minute and crying the next.

Apart from the cost of printing the book, all proceeds go to the Essex Wildlife Trust. To maximise this contribution the book has been published privately, thus cutting out payments that would have otherwise gone to the literary agent, the publisher and the shop. It is only available via EWT Visitor Centres and Waterstone's in Brentwood, but if you have any difficulty finding a copy, or would like to make any comments or corrections, please do not hesitate to contact:

John Cannell on 01277 217236 or john.cannell2@btinternet.com

or

Fiona Agassiz on 01277 230436 or fionaagassiz@hotmail.com

Alternatively come to Warley Place on a Monday morning and ask any of the volunteers.

The price is £5, or £6 including post and packing.

'Well, knowing Mrs Johnson, I'm sure she looks after you very well,' he said as he wound the bandage round Don's arm to take his blood pressure. 'This will go tight for a moment.'

He scribbled down some meaningless figures on his pad, released the pressure and unwound the bandage.

'Well Mr Johnson, there's nothing physically wrong with you,' he said as he settled himself back in his chair. 'But you've got all the symptoms of an anxiety neurosis. Are you sure there's nothing worrying you?'

'You mean I should pull myself together?'

'No, not at all. Funnily enough that can be the best advice for some people, but not for you. What aren't you telling me?'

'Nothing. Retirement is more of a problem than I would have thought. I seem to get in the way rather.'

'I'm sure you don't. But don't worry about it, that won't do either of you any good. I'll prescribe some tablets for you. They may make your mouth a bit dry and they may make you a bit drowsy. And don't drink alcohol while you are taking them. See how you get on and come back and see me in two weeks.'

Don took the prescription, almost forgot to thank him in his haste to get out, and ran across the road to the chemist.

Thank God it was only nerves, he thought as stood waiting for the girl to call his name. For Christ's sake get a move on, can't you? Unable to keep still and worrying about getting in people's way he wandered over to a clear spot and stood staring blankly at some shelves.

'Excuse me!' said a woman pointedly and as he moved aside he realised he had been looking at some very personal women's items. He felt his face grow hot, which embarrassed him even more.

'Mr Johnson?'

Oh God, she'll wonder why I'm all red.

'That's me.'

'Number Twenty-nine Brooklands Avenue?'

'Yes.'

He almost grabbed the packet from her and ran out of the shop, looking at his watch for the tenth time in five minutes.

The girl smiled.

'He certainly needs those,' she said to the pharmacist at the back of the shop as she watched him run back across the road and down the alley. 'Some people never learn.'

A few minutes later, breathing heavily, he was letting himself in.

Susan appeared.

'You said you would get in early,' she said despairingly.

'Yes but...'

'Oh well. Where's the wine?'

He froze. 'Oh! I forgot, I'll get it now.'

She shut her eyes, then turned away dabbing at them with a handkerchief, her lips trembling.

'I really am sorry,' he called after her. 'I've been to the doctor's. We've got time before Margaret and George get here.'

'That was lovely dear,' he said as they all settled back to coffee and After Eights. And it had been pleasant. Margaret and George were very fond of each other and easy to get on with. He wished he and Susan could be like that, but it seemed hardly likely at the moment. Approaching seventy, George still had a fine head of hair, although completely white, and a nice well trimmed moustache that complemented his military bearing, and a wealth of interesting tales that always left Donald disappointed when it was time for them to go. Margaret too had worn well, a few inches shorter than her husband and perhaps having to watch her figure more carefully, she was someone you listened to. She had a much softer appearance than her sister, he thought. A more rounded face, fuller mouth, less severe hair style.

Susan had been a bit subdued, he mused, but appearances were everything to her so you could hardly tell from her manner that there had been anything seriously wrong.

'Where are you going for your holidays this year?' asked George.

Oh sod it.

'Ah – ' Donald started to say.

'Scotland,' said Susan. 'Don booked it. Then probably Spain as usual later on.'

'Scotland?' said Margaret. 'Oh George, can't we go there again?'

'You've been there?' asked Donald. 'When was that?'

'Too many years ago now,' laughed George. 'We stayed in a place called Oban and toured around the west coast. Must be the best scenery in Europe, right on our doorstep. We've never seen anything like it, have we dear?'

'No, it's beautiful,' said Margaret. 'Stay in Glasgow on the way and' – she turned to Susan – 'make sure he takes you round the shops. Buchanan Street, that's where you must go. And the Barras. Oh I wish we were coming with you. And the Cantonese restaurants round by the University...'

Oh bugger, thought Don as he considered the turn of events.

'Yes, but – '

'What about the midges?' cut in Susan, brightening up a little.

'Well we had heard about them, but neither of us was troubled by them. Best to be prepared though.'

'But –'

'Was it cold?'

'Well we didn't go there to sunbathe. It was just right for touring. We had one wet day, but it didn't matter much, we just went round indoor things that day. But you could always take anoraks and things.'

'I keep trying to say,' Donald burst out. There was silence. 'I cancelled it this afternoon. You really didn't want to go dear and there was no point in paying all that money for you to be miserable.'

'It wasn't that I didn't want to go,' retorted Susan, her eyes wide. 'I was just surprised, that was all. We hadn't discussed it and you came in and said that was where we were going.'

'Plenty of time next year,' broke in a now worried looking George. 'In fact it will be better if you have more time to plan where to go and what to do. I thoroughly recommend it though.'

'We really must go now Susan dear,' said Margaret, looking at her watch. 'Long drive home. Thanks for a lovely evening.'

Donald didn't need to look at his watch to know how early in the evening it was.

Waving goodbye as they drove off, he shut the front door.

'They're a nice couple,' he said as they made their way into the kitchen to clear up, now their visitors had gone.

His stomach sank at the stony silence.

He felt the tension rising. The sound of the plates as they were put into the dishwasher echoed through his head.

'I've got to take these pills,' he said when the dishwasher was full. 'I'd better sleep in the spare room in case I disturb you.'

'Right,' she said, not arguing.

She walked quickly upstairs to get ready for bed, while he busied himself with locking doors and windows.

His stomach was churning. He went to his coat and took out the little bottle. Oh well, nothing to lose by trying them, he thought. In fact, what the hell, I'll take two.

By the time he got upstairs she was in bed and her door shut. His pyjamas were on the bed in the spare room. God damn the woman, he thought. I can't do anything right. I am going to Warley Place. Definitely, I don't care what she says. Gordon is right. I have to be more assertive.

Teeth brushed, a quick wash, and he was pulling back the sheets. A movement by the radiator caught his eye and a huge spider crawled along the skirting board.

Seconds was all it took to get a glass from the bathroom and trap the spider beneath it. He slipped a piece of paper under the glass and picking them both up, crept along the landing to the other bedroom. Carefully he put the glass down by the door and withdrew the paper. Then he lifted the glass, and with a flick of his fingers sent the creature scurrying into Susan's room.

Contented, he went back to his bed. The pills worked quickly and he was fast asleep within a minute or two. Dead to the world, he never heard his wife pleading with him to remove the dreadful spider that was watching her from its vantage point over the wardrobe.

10

Wherein Jacob becomes acquainted with Alex

'My God!' exclaimed Alex as he and Jacob stopped on the little bridge over the gorge. 'I've never seen anything like it!'

'It's the alpine garden,' said Jacob, making no attempt to hide his pleasure at his companion's surprise. The deep gorge, passing about ten or twelve feet below them, had been formed to take a small stream from an upper pond to the lower, passing through this artificial valley on the way. Framed by huge rocks brought down from Yorkshire by James Backhouse and Son, who had also carried out the excavation and construction work and planned the garden with Ellen Willmott, it was indeed a picture of delight at this time of the year. Jacob knew that Alex had no idea what the plants were that seemed to cover the sides of the valley, nor that they came from all parts of the world and only grew here because of the care that had been taken in fashioning their home and in caring for them during weather that would otherwise have finished them off. Some were small and delicate-looking, others tall and strong, all beautiful even to an untutored eye.

'What's that?' asked Alex, pointing towards to a glistening surface at ground level some hundred feet away alongside the stream.

'That is the filmy fern cave,' explained Jacob. 'Some of the rarer ferns just would not survive in the open so we constructed a special cave for them. A side-stream runs through it to the pond, keeping it moist, and the glass roof keeps it warm.'

'Where do they come from then?'

'Well some of them from as far away as you can get. *Trichomanes cruentium* and *reniforme* both come from New Zealand for instance, though *Hymenophylum tunbridgense* comes from much closer – Westmoreland in fact.'

'Why do you refer to your plants by their Latin names all the time?' asked Alex. 'Why can't you just call them dandelions, or buttercups, or whatever? It would be much less confusing.'

Jacob smiled. This was an argument he had heard many times before.

'Less confusing for you, possibly – if one could think up enough names for them all. For instance we have twenty-five kinds of Primula here. Finding meaningful common names for all of them would be very difficult. We have about forty Campanulas. The same applies to them.'

'Very well, I accept that, but the Latin names are just as confusing.'

'Not once you get used to them. Are you familiar with *Primula sikkimensis*?' asked Jacob.

'Well, I've heard of Primulas,' replied Alex somewhat doubtfully. 'They're primroses, aren't they?'

Jacob smiled.

'A primrose is a primula, yes. But a primula may also be, say, a cowslip.'

'So *Primula* is the name of a family of flowers?'

'Very good. But no, not quite correct. *Primula* is a genus belonging to the family *Primulaceae*.'

'So what is the difference between a Genus and a Family? Other than as you say, one being further up the botanic order than the other?'

Jacob looked at Alex. Now his mind was occupied he seemed so much more relaxed. Normally assistants were just told what to do and not encouraged to ask questions, but Alex was worth more than that.

'First of all notice the similar names of the genus *Primula* and the family *Primulaceae*. Usually the family name is derived from one of its member genera – the plural of genus – with *aceae* added. In this case primula already has an 'a' at the end, so we don't add a second one so the family becomes *Primulaceae*.'

'That could be confusing.'

'Yes, it can for the beginner but you soon get used to it.'

'So how do plants fit into a particular family or genus?'

'They do usually have similar characteristics, but it's actually a lot more complicated than that and not always as precise a method of differentiating as one would like. I think we'd better skip that one for now.'

'Then what is a species?'

'My goodness, you are a glutton for information. A species is a group of plants that can interbreed.'

'Ranking below genus?'

'Excellent, yes, below genus.
'Right, so it's Family, Genus, Species in that order.'
Jacob groaned.
'What's the matter?' asked a puzzled Alex.
'Well I didn't tell you the names of all the taxonomic categories.'
'Oh, so that's what they are called.' A smile lit up his face. 'Don't tell me. One of the other categories is an order.'
'That's right. The main categories, in the sequence from largest to smallest, are Kingdom (one of which is plants), Division, Class, Order, Family, Subfamily, Genus and Species. *Please* don't ask me to explain what they all are because some of them require a knowledge of botany which you may not have acquired yet.'
He looked at Alex, and added 'But I have no doubt you soon will.'
Why was it that Alex was so interested in the botanic details? Was it that his mind was like a vacuum at present, soaking up knowledge to fill the gaps? Or was it that it was a nice safe subject that took his mind off what was really bothering him?
'Now answer a question from me,' continued Jacob. 'Which one of those plants is the *Primula sikkimensis*?'
Alex looked in bewilderment at the array of plants spread out in front of him extending down to the bottom of the deep cut gorge, amongst the rocks and along the sides.
'That one?' he guessed. 'It's yellow and primroses are yellow. On the other hand it does seem rather taller than a primrose.'
'Not bad at all,' said Jacob admiringly. 'We'll make a gardener of you in no time at all. And its name?'
'I suppose the scent makes men sick?'
Jacob chuckled.
'No, it comes from Sikkim. That's a Kingdom in the Himalayas, between Nepal and Bhutan. Miss Willmott is fond of collecting plants from far off places and I am equally fond of tending to them. The ending *'ensis'* denotes the place of origin or growth, in this case the origin is Sikkim so it is called *sikkimensis*.'
'But what happens if later on they find that it really originated somewhere else, in this case say Afghanistan?'

55

'That's a good point,' said Jacob, impressed. 'In that case I'm afraid the name sticks.'

Alex nodded. 'And what is that one?' he said, pointing to a shrub about five feet tall and eight feet across, with large pink blooms.

'No,' said Jacob. 'If I tell you too many names you will forget all of them. One at a time is best. You will remember *Primula sikkimensis*. Another one tomorrow.'

'Please?'

'My goodness you are persistent. Very well, it is a *Cistus purpureus*. The 'purpureus' just refers to the purple eye it has on the base of each petal – you can't see that from here. You will be delighted to know that this one does have a common name – the Purple Rockrose. But before you say that proves your point, another thing to remember when you use common names is that they often refer to different plants in different parts of the world. Bluebells, for instance, can refer to four different plants. But *Hyancinthoides non-scripta* will mean the same to everyone everywhere.'

'All right, I am convinced,' laughed Alex. 'But it will take a long time to learn them all. Can we have a look in the cave?'

'Most certainly, but not now.'

'What can I do to help then?'

'Miss Willmott has suggested that you work on repairing the wall of the walled garden. Some of the bricks are loose and it needs repointing. I will show you how to do it but it is a boring job so every so often you can come over here and help me with the plants.'

'How did you learn about plants then Jacob?'

'From Henri Correvon.'

On seeing Alex's blank look, he continued.

'I'm Swiss, you see.'

'That explains it. I guessed you weren't from Warley!'

'I worked as a young man for Henri Correvon at his Jardin d'Acclimatation in Geneva. Miss Willmott knew Henri quite well and they agreed that I could come and work here. I had heard of her plans for an alpine garden and it was an opportunity I just could not turn down. That was in 1894, twenty-five years ago. Things are difficult now, but before the war it was a fantastic place to be working. Do you know we had about a hundred gardeners working here at one time?'

Alex looked about and tried to imagine what it must have been like with so many people bustling about watering, pulling up weeds, mowing the lawn, pruning and whatever else it was that gardeners did. Now it would have been quite easy to work on one's own and not see another soul all day. He wondered what it was that kept Jacob there.

'Are you married?' he asked Jacob.

Jacob felt a lump appearing in his throat as he recalled his beloved Rosina.

'She died last year.'

'Oh I am sorry.'

'It's all right, I am getting over it. And I have nine children to worry about.'

'Nine?! Where do they stay?'

'In the South Lodge.'

'That little place by the gate? All of you, in there?'

'It's not so bad. And you? Don't you remember anything about your past?'

'I was a pilot, I think. But I hated it. I liked flying, but I hated killing. If I try to think any deeper there is a wall and I just can't get past it. I don't know that I want to. Now talking about walls, what about the one that needs fixing? I've never done any bricklaying but I'm happy to have a go.'

'It's quite easy once you get the hang of it, but surprisingly difficult until you do, if that makes sense,' said Jacob as they made their way to the shed. You won't have to do any bricklaying yet, just repair the mortar where it has come loose or fallen out. We make our mortar with lime, not this new fangled cement. Three parts of sand to one of lime. I will show you how, but first you will need to clean the old damaged mortar out.'

He pulled out a bag containing what looked like a small ice axe, a hammer and a chisel, trowels, a brush and a dust sheet and handed them to Alex.

'Just do this area for the moment,' suggested Jacob, showing Alex an area about ten bricks wide and ten high where the mortar really was crumbling badly. He very carefully laid the dust sheet down over the flowers before starting to chip at the mortar

57

between two bricks with the axe to get the worst stuff out, then chiselled it clear before passing the equipment to Alex.

He stood back while Alex carefully extended the cavity along several more bricks, before then chiselling them clear as Jacob had done.

'Why are the bricks so different?' he asked. 'I can see thin ones, thick ones, red ones, yellow ones. And they all look pretty old.'

'There are bricks here that are two hundred years old,' came a voice from behind a huge *Ceanothus coerulea*. 'And that is the way I like them.'

'What you must do,' said Ellen Willmott as she emerged and came up to them, 'is to make sure that you clear the underside of the upper brick. Otherwise the mortar will come out. Give me the chisel.'

She bent down and looked up into the crevice.

'Not bad for someone who has not done this work before, but just a little more needs to be removed.'

She inserted the chisel angled upwards and in a series of sharp blows with the mallet cleared more debris out.

'Do them all like that and it will be fine,' she said, moving back to her *Ceanothus*.

'Was that really necessary?' whispered Alex.

'You've just been paid a compliment, believe it or not,' replied Jacob. 'Usually she would stand over someone and make sure they did what she told them before she moved away. She has enough confidence in you not to bother.'

Jacob busied himself in the walled garden, well away from Ellen Willmott, for half an hour until Alex called him over. Pleased to see that Alex had already brushed out the dust, he ran his finger along the underside of the bricks.

'That's fine I think,' he said, glancing at Ellen Willmott and seeing her nod her acceptance. 'Now we will mix a little mortar.'

They walked back to the shed and mixed a small amount of sand and lime on a big board, then added water until it was like a thick paste. Alex shovelled it into an old bucket and carried it back to the wall.

Jacob picked up the mortar board and slopped some mixture on it, then holding it close to the wall packed some mortar into the space using a small trowel.

'Here, you have a go,' he said.

Alex took the board and trowel and pushed some of the mixture into the gap, smoothing it with his trowel, then stepped back.

'Oh dear,' he said.

Jacob laughed. 'Not so easy, is it? Never mind, have a go at the rest. When you've finished I'll show you how to get the mortar off the bricks and how to get a nice even finish to the pointing.'

Alex tried again with the next brick with only a marginal improvement.

'Sorry Jacob, but I will get the hang of it. I'm worried about spoiling the bricks though.'

'Don't worry about the bricks,' said Ellen Willmott, back again. 'Jacob will show you how to dress it up afterwards, when it has dried a little but not set. You are doing all right. I am going in now for a while Jacob.'

'Does she always creep up on you like that?' asked Alex as Ellen Willmott left the garden and went in through the conservatory.

'Quite often,' laughed Jacob. 'You get used to it. She must like you though.'

At that moment the distant sound of an aeroplane broke the silence and Jacob was horrified to see the change in expression as Alex's eyes opened wide and then shut tight, only opening again when the aeroplane fortunately went on its way without coming too close.

'When you are ready,' said Jacob softly, 'you can tell me everything. If you want to, that is.'

But Alex's expression had changed completely. His forehead was creased in a puzzled frown that gradually cleared to a look of complete peace.

Jacob stopped and listened. He could just make out Ellen Willmott's voice coming from the Music Room.

'That's The Last Rose of Summer,' Jacob said as she finished. 'She only sings the first verse because –'

'Because she thinks the others are too sad,' said Alex.

Jacob glanced at him, then quickly looked away when he saw the tears trickling down Alex's cheeks.

11

To Warley Place

I'm going to Warley this morning,' he said hesitantly. 'I'll try not to be late back.'

'Do you need to take anything to eat? You'll be hungry after all that hard work.'

He couldn't believe it. After all their arguments she was actually concerned about his welfare.

'I was going to come home for lunch.'

'What do the rest of them do?'

'They take sandwiches and a drink. Then they sometimes finish jobs off after lunch, but if not they go home.'

'Well you don't want to be different. I'll make up some sandwiches.'

'Thanks.'

Donald went to the shed and collected his overalls, boots and gloves and took them out to the car. What on earth had happened? She hadn't been this friendly for years.

'I'm looking forward to meeting the others,' he said as he came back in. 'They are all retired professional people.'

'So you said.' He could see that she was just a bit impressed. Perhaps that was why she was happier about it. 'Well if I read about brick walls falling down at Warley Place I'll know who is to blame!' She was definitely pleased that he was going. Perhaps she was pleased to see the back of him.

She passed him his sandwiches and a thermos flask of coffee.

'Thanks dear.'

As he opened the door he felt a warmth towards her that he hadn't felt for years. He turned and smiled.

'See you later then.'

'Take care.'

He could hardly believe it as she stood at the door and waved him off before going back inside.

Having left Brentwood and with a brief stretch of open road behind him, he slowed down at the 30 mph sign and passed the long wall on his right before coming to the junction of three roads. He took a deep breath and swung his car to the right as Gordon had told him, bisecting two of them and hoping that nothing would come speeding round the bend ahead or out of the *Thatchers Arms* public house as he did so. Coming to a stop at a forbidding looking gate, he sat there for a moment, wondering why on earth anyone would have an entrance at such a dangerous junction: Presumably because it wasn't always dangerous, not in the days of horses and carts. For this was a very old site indeed. Gordon had said that the gate would be open, but chatting with Susan had made him a bit late.

Suddenly remembering that others may also want to enter on this fine Monday morning, he got out of his Ford Focus to open the creaky barrier. As it swung back he grinned at the notice, which asked users to make sure the gate was shut when entering or leaving the site. How could anyone enter or leave the site with the gate shut? Try not to make too many wisecracks, he told himself. Other people don't always appreciate them. It was all right when he was working, but now he was retired he'd have to be careful.

He looked up over the fence as he pushed the gate fully open. There in front of him was a small single storey cottage. The white-painted clapboard construction provided the perfect backdrop for the diamond pattern lattice windows either side of the front door. It seemed older than the cedar shingle roof and the single chimney would suggest. It was a bit neglected, especially the garden, but had a peculiar beauty that he couldn't explain.

Back in his car he got, drove through the opening and obediently got out and shut the gate behind him before driving on down the narrow tree-lined lane and then left on to a small car park, shaded by yet more trees. In fact there were trees as far as he could see. He resolved to buy himself a field guide, otherwise he could see himself looking rather silly not knowing one from another. Horse chestnuts were OK, as long as they had conkers on them. Same applied to sweet chestnuts with their prickly fruit pods. Oh yes, oaks were easy with acorns and sycamores with the winged seeds that he used to play with as a boy. But that was about it. Yes, a book on trees was a priority.

So this was Warley Place. He'd read about it in an Essex Wildlife Trust booklet that Gordon had given him so that he wouldn't seem too ignorant.

61

The estate was once part of the Manor of Warley Abbess, the property of Barking Abbey until the Dissolution; he remembered that. When was The Dissolution? He had meant to look it up but had forgotten to do so; four hundred years ago, something like that. One thing was sure – this place was very old.

It was the famous Miss Willmott who had really put it on the map, much later on. Well, Gordon had told him she was famous, but he had to admit to never having heard of her before. The Willmott family apparently lived there from 1875 until 1934 and during that time she became a renowned botanist and plantswoman, transforming the gardens into something wonderful in the process. But then she died, and with no direct descendents to occupy it, the property became derelict. The house was pulled down just before the Second World War and the gardens were allowed to grow into a jungle. All that remained were the rather decrepit walls of the walled garden, a ruined conservatory and the remains of a coach house. The rest was just foundations to remind visitors of what had been there and some remnants of the exotic plants she had lovingly nurtured.

In recent times part of the estate had been leased to the Essex Wildlife Trust, who now managed it. Donald had already forgotten the names of the warden and the assistant warden who looked after the enthusiastic group of volunteers each Monday. They were mostly retired people apparently, men and women, and wanting the exercise and with an interest in conservation.

Drawing up alongside half a dozen other cars he got out and looked about. A couple of men were wheeling a barrow full of tools up the main driveway. Two or three were rummaging about in a shed tucked away in the trees. Three more were poring over a map of some sort.

'Hi there,' came a friendly voice, and he turned to see a smiling woman in an old anorak striding towards him. 'Have you come to help?'

'I certainly have, if I can. Don't know anything about plants though. Gordon told me about it and I wondered if I could help.'

'There are lots of other things to do. Bricklaying and pointing, for instance.'

'I'm afraid I don't know how to do that either.'

'You soon will! My name's Daphne by the way. Gordon's gone on ahead.'

'I'm Donald.'

'Have you got any boots or gloves?'

'Oh yes, Gordon told me what to bring.'

She waited patiently while Donald pulled his overalls on, tied up the laces on his working boots and picked up his bag with drinks, sandwiches and gloves. She then led him through yet another gate and up a driveway no more than six or eight feet wide comprising a stone pathway edged with what looked like long poles split down the middle. On either side were yet more interesting looking trees and rhododendrons. He could just see a field through them on one side, foundations of a building poking through the almost impenetrable forest on the other.

'This used to be the main road to Brentwood,' Daphne commented. 'The pilgrims used it on their way to Canterbury. The bypass was put in before the Willmotts came though.'

'What's that little cottage by the gate?' asked Donald. 'Is it part of the estate?'

'That's where Jacob Maurer once lived – with a wife and nine children! But although it used to be part of Ellen Willmott's estate, no, it isn't included in the bit administered by Essex Wildlife Trust.'

'Good grief! Who was Jacob Maurer?'

'Oh, he was the chap Ellen Willmott got in from Switzerland to develop the alpine garden. The rocks and the gorge are still there, but hardly any of the original plants.'

'That's a shame. Any idea what I will be doing?'

'I'm sure Ben will find something.'

Such a lot to learn, thought Donald.

'Who is Ben?'

'Assistant Warden. He sorts out jobs for everyone. You'll like him. Frank's here too, he's the warden, but he usually leaves organising the work parties to Ben.'

'How many come?'

'Oh, it varies. On a good day about twenty. If it's a bit wet maybe eight or ten. About a dozen today.'

A minute and two corners later and they came to a stop in front of a couple of wiry weatherbeaten men somewhat older than Donald but looking an awful lot fitter. The shorter of the two had a flat cap, the taller one greying hair open to the elements. One thing they had in common was that each had a pair of secateurs hung in a holster on his belt, for all the world like a sheriff and his deputy with six-guns on their hips trying to get a posse together.

'Donald, this is Ben and Frank.'

They both smiled a greeting.

'Donald has come to help. He's a friend of Gordon's. Have you got a job for him Ben?'

'Right, er, hello Donald. Done any bricklaying?'

'No, sorry.'

'No matter, you can help on the wall.'

'But – '

Ben strode off, Donald following wondering what on earth he had got himself into.

Round two more corners they went, over a rough path through the endless trees, leaving him tripping over roots and thoroughly lost. Suddenly they strode through a gap in a rather tall wall and he stopped and gasped. It was a walled garden. But what a walled garden! About fifty metres long, almost forty metres wide, surrounded by a wall that seemed three metres high. Even he recognised the magnolia tree, if only because it was in bloom, but he had no idea what the others were. The same applied to the flowers and shrubs growing round the trees. What must it have been like in its glory days?

He realised Ben had stopped and was grinning at him.

'Sorry Ben,' he said, hurrying to catch up. 'It's fantastic!'

'Yes, but it won't be much longer if we don't repair the wall. Mostly re-pointing, but some rebuilding where it needs it. Haven't you been round the gardens then?'

'No, not yet,' Donald replied to Ben's back as he scurried after him.

They came to a part of the wall where a primitive wooden scaffolding had been set up. Two people were up there already, pushing mortar in where the old crumbling material had been scraped or had fallen out.

'Ian, Carla, this is Donald.'

'What did you do to deserve this, rob a bank?' asked Ian.

'Are you mad?' asked Carla. 'Coming here?'

'They love it really,' said Ben.

'But those bricks,' said Donald. 'They're all different sizes. And that mortar, it doesn't look like normal mortar.'

'It isn't. The bricks are very old. Ellen Willmott didn't like new bricks. And the mortar has lime in it to make it more pliable and to fit in with the old lime mortar. The old stuff is quite soft – too soft for safety these days, but suitable for the soft bricks that were used then – but it's just as well for you because you'll be scraping it out for these two to put new stuff in.'

'So is that what we use then?'

'No, we put some cement in to make it a bit harder and quicker to set. I'll show you when we do the next mix. Meanwhile, get chipping.'

He pulled out of an enormous bag a vicious looking tool that looked like an ice-axe. Taking the axe, he chipped away between some bricks for a few minutes, explaining how it should be done to enable the new mortar to stick properly. Make sure the upper edge of the opening was really clean so the mortar would stay in properly, brush the dust off afterwards, clean off any loose bricks before replacing them.

'Right?'

'Er, no, not really,' said Donald. 'I think you'll have to show me for a bit longer. Say a couple of hours. When's tea break?'

'You'll fit in here well,' chuckled Ben. 'If you live long enough.'

Yes, thought Donald. I'm going to like it here. It was a long time since he had felt like making light hearted remarks.

'Welcome to the gang,' said Carla as Ben wandered off and Donald started tentatively chipping away at the old mortar.

'Thanks.'

She seems very pleasant, he thought. A trace of an accent though. Scandinavian perhaps. Most of the volunteers were of retirement age, but the women he'd seen seemed a few years younger than the men. One thing they all had in common was a very pleasant disposition.

'When are you off to Germany?' Ian asked Carla.

'I'm off next week actually,' she said. 'For six weeks.'

'Don't worry, we'll keep it for you until you get back!'

There was quiet for a bit while Donald chipped and scraped at the mortar and a haze of dust gradually enveloped him.

'Whoops,' he said as a brick suddenly came loose with a big lump of mortar. 'Does that matter? A brick just came out.'

'No, there's lots of loose ones. It's actually a double wall, bricks each side with rubble filling the gap, so it happens quite a lot. We just mortar them back in again. Strip the old stuff away round it and leave the brick in the hole.'

It didn't seem long before a whistle blew.

'Tea break,' explained Carla, climbing down and picking up her bag. Donald grabbed his own and followed the two of them back to the only covered area on the site, apart from the two bird hides. It consisted of four rather old walls covered by some corrugated plastic to keep the rain off. It was rather optimistically labelled 'Display Area' and apart from some rough and ready benching contained interesting old plans and photographs pinned to the walls.

'OK?' asked Ben as Donald found a space and fished out a cold drink from his bag. 'This is Donald,' he announced to the other dozen sitting about.

'Hi,' came the response and he immediately forgot every single one of the names that were offered to him. Apart from Gordon's of course. Gordon had been pulling stinging nettles and was rubbing some red patches on his arms.

'He's got you chipping out the mortar then,' one of them grinned, looking at Donald's overalls now covered in white powder.

'Yes,' said Donald mournfully. 'It's lime mortar too.'

'Yes, that's right,' said Ben.

'What if he get Lyme's Disease?' asked Gordon.

'Oh God!' groaned one. It was Frank, the warden, Donald noticed.

'What's Lime's Disease?' asked another, puzzled.

'Lyme Disease is what you can get from ticks Norman,' Frank explained. 'It's spelt with a 'y', nothing to do with lime in mortar.'

'Oh. A pun then.'

'Yes,' said Ben. 'And he'll be pulling nettles until he stops making them.'

'A sort of PUNishment?' suggested Gordon.

'Who let him in?' asked someone else.

After some chat about the various plants and the progress generally, people started drifting back to their various jobs. It was interesting to see how keen they all were to get things finished, rather than let the break drag on.

'Are you OK doing that?' asked Ben, as Donald picked up his hammer again.

'Fine. It's quite relaxing.'

'We'll find you something different to do next week, it's a filthy job.'

'No, I don't mind, really.'

'So you haven't been round here before?'

'No. I don't know why, but no, I haven't.'

Ben looked at his watch.

'I've got to go back to the store. Come on, we'll go the long way round and I'll show you the terrace and the gorge. We can look at the rest next week.'

Donald followed Ben out of the garden and back past the outside of the wall. Edging down a short slope past a 'danger' notice he stopped.

'This is the terrace,' he announced.

Donald stood there, his mouth open. The terrace itself had been cut into a natural slope, the earth being held back by a wall a couple of metres high. The wall seemed about thirty metres long, the centre of it jutting out with steps leading down both ways to the lower level. One wall was obviously new, though built in the old style. The other wall was in the process of being rebuilt. The centre part and the steps were badly in need of repair. Water butts, packets of sand, mixing boards, trestles, all manner of building materials scattered about.

'That's going to be brilliant when it's finished!' he said.

Ben chuckled. 'Come on, I'll show you the gorge.'

Off they wandered, down a path past a little open fronted brick building and some huge chestnut trees, until they came to a small footbridge over a miniature ravine about two or three metres deep. It was bordered by enormous rocks.

'This used to be Ellen Willmott's alpine garden,' explained Ben. 'It's dry now, but there used to be a stream running down there. And over there was a cave, built for her ferns.'

'Daphne told me about this,' said Donald. 'It must have been quite a sight when it was full of flowers. There's a sort of eerie feeling about the place. All of it, really, but this bit in particular.'

'A lot of people have said that.'

They crossed the bridge and a few minutes later were back on the driveway.

'Now are you sure you don't mind doing some more chipping?'

'Perfectly sure.'

'And can you find your way back without getting lost?' he laughed.

'I'll try!'

Ben wandered off, satisfied. It was good to see how concerned he was, thought Donald, as he retraced his steps back to the wall to continue with his work.

What with the almost hypnotic sound of the hammer and the cheerful conversation with Carla and Ian, the time flew by and a couple of hours later they were once more in the little display area, this time for lunch.

With relief Donald found that the conversation did not revolve round football, but involved such things as rotary engines and a recent metal detector survey of some of the site.

'Right, no point in making up any more mortar,' said Ian. 'I think I'll call it a day.'

'Me too,' said Carla. 'I've got to get ready for my holiday.'

'Oh yes, we'll miss you, but your wall will be waiting when you get back,' said Ben.

She grinned, put her bag over her shoulder, and made for the car park with Ian.

'I'll just do a bit more,' said Donald, getting to his feet. 'When do we finish?'

'Oh, people start drifting away now,' said Frank. 'Some stay until four o'clock, most go about three.'

Donald wandered back to the wall, content. He knew he was going to enjoy himself here each Monday. Picking up the hammer he started to chip. Another loose brick! He pulled it out and hooked at the loose mortar. The brick next to it came out too. He bent down and lifted a brush from the toolbag, then carefully reached in and brushed the dust and bits of mortar away to clear the opening.

He stopped suddenly. At the back of the gap, where the rubble infill should have been, there was something smooth. It looked like a package. He reached in, wiggled it free, and pulled it clear. It was a flat parcel, wrapped in what looked like well greased oilskin. He turned round to call Ben, but there was no-one about. He stopped and thought for a moment. After another quick look round he slipped it into his bag. Perhaps he'd look at it first. He'd show it to the others later.

12

Miss Willmott confides in James Robinson regarding Personal matters and speaks to Alex

Ellen Willmott sat in the conservatory looking out at, but hardly seeing, the lawns, the rose pergola and the trees shielding the southern part of the alpine garden and the South Pond. The setting of the sun on this quiet still day reflected her mood as she turned to her companion.

'You must have been here, what, thirty years now James?'

'Indeed I have.'

James Robinson had been appointed by Frederick Willmott, Ellen's father, in the year eighteen-ninety and had served faithfully and well ever since. His role had gradually changed from being a butler to *major-domo*, the only problem being that as his responsibilities increased the resources available to him seemed to decrease in direct proportion. That he took it all in his stride without complaint was to his great credit. It never seemed to occur to Ellen Willmott how much she took him for granted in this role. In fact she appeared to live her life taking everyone and everything for granted. Even the diminishing of her funds she put down to the war, the inadequacies of the publishers of her masterpiece *The Genus Rosa*, her bankers' incompetence, anything but her own naivety in assuming that the supply of sufficient funds to do whatever she wanted would continue unabated.

But the one thing she did not underestimate was James Robinson's value as a confidant. His quiet sense of humour, loyalty and trustworthiness were beyond price.

'It's falling apart James. Where did I go wrong?'

'The past is inscribed in stone,' he said softly. 'Or in your case written with beautiful plants in good soil. There is little point in dwelling on what might have been.'

'But what can I do now?'

'Selling Tresserve and Boccanegra will help.'

She transferred her gaze back to the window, offering no immediate comment. The chateau in France, with its extensive estate, had been purchased in the same year that Robinson had started at Warley; Boccanegra, in Italy, had followed fifteen years later. She had put such a lot of hard work into bringing them to their current beautiful state. She couldn't lose them now, it wasn't fair. But if it was the only way to save Warley...

'I suppose so,' she whispered eventually. 'I just hope that I do not have to sell Warley too!'

James Robinson didn't answer. None was wanted. The possibility had occurred to him also, but surely it was unthinkable?

They sat there in silence for a while.

'What do you think of the new fellow, Alex I think his name is.'

'I have little to do with him, he's always busy in the garden. Have you asked Jacob? I've noticed them talking together on a few occasions. He certainly puts his back into his job.'

'I know all that,' said Ellen rather huffily. 'But you hear things that perhaps I would not.'

'I think not. They can see us clearly now through the windows and know that anything I hear will be passed on to you.'

She knew he was right and almost admitted as such. Almost, but not quite. She contented herself with continuing her gaze over her beloved garden.

'From what I have seen though...'

She smiled to herself. He was a good man, James Robinson.

'... he seems to be well educated and good mannered, not born and bred that way, more learned than natural. And, so I hear, probably having some musical talent.'

'I don't disagree, but can you tell me how you arrived at that conclusion?'

'Well I have to admit to having been curious enough to have gone out into the garden on one or two occasions to converse with him. He shows a great interest in all things, is comfortable pronouncing the latin names of your plants – how accurately I am unable to judge myself – and is ready to admit that he has much to learn and that he might be wrong. The latter humility is a mark of the educated man rather than one born to his position.'

'Very good,' commented Ellen. She also wondered whether the last comment was in some way also directed at her, but dismissed the thought almost as soon as it came.

'And his musical ability?'

'I happened to glance out of an upstairs window when you were singing. It was 'The Last Rose of Summer' as I recall. He was some distance away and my eyes are not what they used to be, but he had seemed upset about something. When you started to sing he was listening intently and seemed to relax. It was as if it meant something to him.'

'Interesting,' she said thoughtfully. 'The other things you have said have all crossed my mind too, but I did not know about the music. Have you any idea what he was upset about?'

'No, I have not.'

'When we are talking like this you may call me Ellen, James. Not when others are present of course, but we have been together for too long for false formality.'

'And too long for me to change,' James Robinson said smiling quietly.

'But avoiding calling me anything is avoiding the issue.'

'It really isn't an issue. But if you insist, will Miss Ellen do?'

She sighed. He would never change.

'Miss Ellen will do. I think something very traumatic happened to him during the war and he is having difficulty coming to terms with it.'

'Something very traumatic happened to many people during the war,' said James. 'Few of those involved will ever be the same again.'

'But this was something exceptional. Something that affected him so much that he has blanked out all memory of it.'

'Perhaps it is best left that way,' suggested James.

'Maybe. But if he is to resume his life as it was he must regain his memory and face its horrors.'

'He might be better off not resuming his life as it was if otherwise he would have to come to terms with what he would rather forget. Isn't that best left to Dr Townsend and his staff at the asylum?'

'I think not, James. The staff do their best, but have you been there? The gloomy wards are really depressing and the gaslights, where there are any, seem to make it worse if anything. At least most of the old straw mattresses are now filled with hair, but it can't be clean there or they wouldn't have had typhoid.'

72

The outbreak of typhoid at the asylum had been two years earlier, but it brought back awful memories of Ellen Willmott's youngest sister who died of diphtheria at an early age. A very common disease at the time, but one that she rightly or wrongly always associated with poor sanitation.

'But the awful conditions don't mean that the staff don't know what they are doing? All credit to them for continuing to work in the place.'

'I know that,' she said stiffly. She hated James trying to correct her, especially when he was right. 'But Dr Townsend brought him here because he was not managing to bring about any improvement treating him there.'

'Also perhaps because the conditions did not assist in the rehabilitation of someone of his upbringing.'

'Possibly,' she said eventually. 'Ask him to come in.'

'Now?'

'Yes, now.'

'And will you wish me to stay when he does come?'

'No. Just show him in to the Library.'

He sighed, opened the door and made his way to the figures in the distance.

She also sighed. She really didn't mean to be rude and James Robinson's companionship was important to her, but sometimes he did have to be reminded of his place. She made her way from the Conservatory and passed through the Library to the Drawing Room, waiting for Alex's to arrive.

She heard the sound of their voices, Robinson asking him to wait in the Library, but did not hear him enter. After a few minutes she opened the door joining the two rooms and found him standing with his back to her looking at her books lined up on the shelves. She realised why she had not heard him when she saw that he had taken his boots off in the Conservatory and was standing in old but well-darned socks. She also saw that his hands were clean, no doubt washed in a watering can or the stream and drying naturally on the way here. He had also attempted to smooth down his brown hair. He sensed her presence and turned quickly.

'I am sorry, didn't mean to be nosey,' he said. 'It's a while since I have seen a good book.'

'There is no need to apologise for having an interest in literature,' she said as kindly as possible to put him at ease. Her first impression was correct, he was well read. 'If there is anything you would like to borrow you only have to ask. It would do my heart good to see them appreciated once more. I see you have Paradise Lost in your hand. What do you think of it?'

'I find it a burden to read.' he admitted. 'The message is interesting but Milton is a bit too certain of his beliefs for me. He leaves no room for individual thought or interpretation. I would prefer a Dickens, although he can be a bit depressing at times!'

'My view entirely. There is an interesting analogy between the ousting of Satan from Heaven and our victory over the Kaiser.'

She wondered for a moment if he were going to agree with the poor analogy out of politeness and felt a twinge of disappointment, but to her relief he spoke out.

'There is an analogy of sorts,' he said thoughtfully. 'But those who will suffer most are the innocent victims of both sides, not the perpetrators. And one has to wonder whether this particular Satan will be back!'

'Well said,' she replied, smiling warmly.

He returned her smile. Not deferential, she thought, but polite, well mannered.

'Is my work satisfactory?' he asked.

'Your work is fine,' she assured him. 'From my point of view anyway. Do you have any quarrel with what you are doing?'

'None whatsoever. Jacob has taught me many things about plants already. It is indeed a fascinating subject and I hope to learn more. Repairing the wall is relaxing in its way and certainly necessary, but I have to say it is not my favourite job.'

'Perhaps you do not like it because you have little to learn from it?'

'Perhaps, Miss Willmott. But perhaps also because I fear I am not very good at it!'

She found herself warming very much to this man and wishing she was thirty years younger.

'You have obviously come from a good background,' she commented. 'But of it you remember nothing?'

His face clouded over.

'No, nothing. There is something.... something bad. I may have been a pilot in the war because when an aeroplane comes over I feel this awful feeling of remorse. My memories are locked away as if in a box and I am frightened to open that box. Can you understand that?'

'I can not understand what you and others like you must have gone through in that ghastly war,' she said, shuddering. 'But I know it must have been truly dreadful.'

'I do remember that I have always hated killing,' Alex continued. 'So perhaps it was that. The Germans were and are mostly no different from us, they just had different leaders. It is such a pity that so few can lead so many to death and destruction.'

'Do you like music?' she asked, perceiving that it was time to move on before he closed in on himself.

'I do,' he said. 'At least, I think I do.'

'Come this way,' she said, walking back into the Conservatory and then into the music room.

As he followed her in she was gratified to hear him gasp as his eyes took in the contents. The organ, the piano, cello, violins...

'This is wonderful!' he gasped. 'Which of them do you play?'

'I play all of them,' she said, her heart lifting. 'Not at the same time of course!'

He laughed.

'Do you play?'

I can play the piano,' he said. 'I think.'

'See what you make of this one,' she said. 'It was a present from my father.'

'But my clothes...I am so dirty.'

'You have washed your hands I see. A bit of good honest dirt on a piano stool won't do any harm.'

He gingerly sat on the stool, lowered it slightly, and rested his hands on the keys.

'Just play whatever comes into your head,' she suggested.

He hesitated for a few seconds, then relaxed and started to play. She was not surprised to find that it was the introduction to one of her songs. She moved to stand behind him and started to sing...

> '*Tis the last rose of summer,*' she sang.
> '*Left blooming all alone.*
> *All her lovely companions are faded and gone.*'

75

He played beautifully and she responded by singing with more feeling than she had done for a long time and was sorry when the last line came.

'To reflect back her blushes or give sigh for sigh.'

'Thank you for playing,' she said, wiping her eyes before he could see that they were a little wet.

He was silent, his back to her. She reached down and laying her hand along his cheek turned his head towards her.

The tears were streaming down his cheeks. He turned in the chair and his voice choking tried to apologise. 'S S Sorry.'

Overcome by compassion for this unfortunate but so loveable person she just put her arms round his shoulders and pulled him to her. She heard the muffled sobs as his body shook. Whatever was it that was hurting him so much?

13

The Journal

Donald looked out of the window. It was too good an evening to stay in. But then he looked back at the package for the hundredth time. He'd been almost too frightened to open it in case whatever was inside had rotted to an unrecognisable mess. But he had to know.

He was still trying to work out why Susan's attitude to his volunteer work had changed. She seemed to have accepted the idea and was more than happy with the idea of him going every Monday. Perhaps it was a talking point with her friends, he wondered. Or his description of some of the people there and what they had done. Telling her that one of them was a doctor was a good move. It was true and impressed her no end. More likely she just wanted to be on her own.

'Go on, open it,' said Susan from her chair, putting the newspaper down. 'It's no good just keeping on looking at it.'

'You're right,' he said. Somehow he felt that if it fell to pieces the responsibility would be shared.

Taking a deep breath he laid out a sheet of brown paper on the coffee table, put the package down on it and carefully peeled back the oilskin. It was still greasy in places, but hard and cracked in others – possibly where the rubble had broken through the protective layer when it had been hidden.

Eventually there in front of him lay a notebook, a bit over four inches wide, say four and a half, and maybe seven inches tall. It was quite thin, not much more than a quarter of an inch. There was nothing written on the front.

He slid the oilskin away, folded it and put it in a plastic bag.

Then, trying to remain calm, he slowly lifted the cover.

The paper was yellow and a bit mouldy looking, and he was disappointed to see that much of the writing was hardly distinguishable. But on the first page he made out, in good well formed handwriting, the words.

'This is my Journal' in large letters, then underneath in smaller script, 'written in 1919 after the Great War'.

'What does it say?'

'It seems to be a journal written by someone just after the First World War,' Donald said to his wife. 'But the paper isn't in good condition and the writing is awful hard to read.'

'You ought to hand it in to someone.'

'I know, dear,' he said. 'But then I wouldn't know what was in it. They'd take ages to copy it down and even then I can't be sure they'd make it public. This way I'll know straight away.'

'But you might damage it and then it would be lost forever.'

'I know you're right Sue. But I found it, and if I hadn't then it would definitely have been lost forever.'

'Even so.'

'Look, I'll be very careful and if I think it is getting damaged I'll do as you say. Meanwhile it's so hard to read I'm going to have to decipher each page and put it on our computer, then we'll both be able to read it more easily and it will be a record in case the worse happens.'

'The worse being?'

'The dog eats it.'

'But we haven't got a dog.'

'I know. That's how unlikely it is that anything will happen to it.'

She laughed. He hadn't heard her laugh properly for a long time.

'Why don't you go back to your crossword?' he suggested good-naturedly. 'This is going to take ages. I'll tell you when I've got anything worth reading or if you can help.'

'I'm stuck. Seven across. *Nine drunk*. Four words, three, four, three, five letters.'

'Oh,' he said absently. He wished he could do crosswords like her. How she had got started on them he'd never know.

'OK, I'll shut up. Anyway, I've just got it.'

'Got what?'

'The answer. It's 'one over the eight'.

'Pardon?'

'Nine is one more than eight. It also means drunk. So that's the answer.'

'Crazy,' muttered Donald as she scribbled the answer in and he carefully lifted the next page. It was a little damp and looked as though it would tear easily, but he eased it off its companion and turned it across the notebook. He stared at the page for a moment and then started entering as many words as he could read. There seemed to be more question marks than words to begin with.

I h?ve d??e a t??ribl? t?ing was presumably *I have done a terrible thing,* that was straightforward enough. Strange that he hadn't said what his name was though. That was the first thing most people would put in a Journal, one would suppose. Fairly easy to translate when letters were indecipherable, but when whole words were like it it posed more of a problem. Perhaps Susan was right. Experts would have special tools for making such things readable. But he'd give it his best shot first. He ploughed on.

'Well, that's the first section done,' he said eventually, straightening up. Looking across for a comment he saw the completed crossword laying there and a cold cup of tea by his elbow. He stretched and rubbed his eyes and looked at the clock. If all the pages were like that it was going to take weeks of solid work to get it all copied out.

'Susan!' he called. 'I'm going to give it a rest. Fancy coming to see where I found the journal?'

She walked in with a cup of tea in her hand.

'Have you finished?'

'No, just the first section. There are several sections, this one started off with a tantalising hint of something interesting, then went on about his early life. Funnily enough he still hasn't said what his name is. Do you fancy going?'

'It's a bit late isn't it? Will it be open?'

'Doesn't shut until dusk so we've got a couple of hours yet. Anyway, I know where the key is.'

'OK then, I'd like to see it.'

Twenty minutes later they were shutting the big gate behind them and taking the car on the hundred yards or so to the little car park, now deserted.

'This is eerie,' whispered Susan as Donald locked the car and they stood listening to the breeze whispering through the leaves. 'Are you sure it won't get dark while we are still in there?'

'No, it'll be fine,' Donald reassured her with a confidence he didn't feel. The sun was very low already and the thick forest of trees with their full complement of leaves meant that in effect dusk was already upon them.

He led her through the second gate and up the drive through the trees and rhododendrons towards the ruined house.

'This used to be the main road to Brentwood until the middle of the nineteenth century,' he whispered.

'Donald.'

'Yes?'

'Why are we whispering?'

'Don't know,' he said, more loudly this time.

'Shhh,' said Susan. 'Don't want to disturb the ghosts.'

They walked quietly through the trees down the drive, then turned left towards the walled garden.

'This is the display area,' he whispered.

'You are whispering again,' said Susan.

'As you say, don't want to disturb the ghosts. Apparently Ellen Willmott still stalks the grounds making sure visitors don't harm her plants.'

'Donald.'

'Yes?'

'You just made that up.'

'Well, she might do. Here, round here, this is the walled garden.'

He couldn't believe how long her good mood was lasting. If only she was always like this! Perhaps it was the new interest. He had to admit that he could be boring at times. This was like one of her crossword puzzles. Clues waiting for an answer.

'That's a palm tree,' she said looking at the Chusan Palm. 'And those magnolias are really good. Oh look, a *Ginkgo biloba* tree!'

'Yes,' he grunted, trying to look as though he already knew what they were and leading her along the wall to the small staging where he and his two colleagues had been repairing the pointing.

'There,' he said, pointing to a couple of bricks. 'That's where I got it. They haven't been mortared back in yet.'

'What a coincidence,' she commented. 'All those bricks and you happen to find the two that the journal was hidden behind.'

'Yes, I suppose it is rather. If it had been one loose brick I probably wouldn't have looked, but two together... I wonder if he

80

perhaps left them badly mortared so that there was a chance it would be found?'

'Possibly. Or perhaps he was disturbed when he was putting them back and had to do it in a hurry.'

'How many of these plants were Ellen Willmott's?' she asked, looking round again at the garden itself.

'No idea. There's a notice over there, we can look at it on the way out. I'd like to find out more about it. But I do know that most of her plants were stripped out when she died. Why don't you come and join the group?'

He regretted suggesting it as the words came out, but she just shook her head.

'No, it's your thing. I'm glad I've seen it though. Oughtn't we to be going now?'

'I'll just show you the terrace that Ben is restoring. It'll be brilliant when it's done.'

They walked back along the wall to the exit from the walled garden and then down the same way along the outside until they came to what amounted to a small building site. The remains of brick walls and steps just about showed that it was once a terrace, with the start of a new retaining wall showing what was being done to restore it to what once must have been a beautiful and peaceful area.

'This is Ben's current baby,' said Donald. 'I think it's going to look brilliant when it's finished. Not much of a view though, with all those trees in the way.'

'They probably weren't there when this was built. I can really imagine Ellen Willmott sitting here.'

'Yes, although for the latter part of her life when it all got rather too much for her I think she concentrated on the walled garden and the alpine garden. The view from here might have been a bit depressing for her, looking at the parts of the garden that weren't being looked after. Come on, let's look at what used to be the alpine garden.'

'Oh, I'm not sure,' said Susan doubtfully, looking at the slope down which Donald was heading. 'It's getting dark. We might have an accident.'

The sun had indeed gone down but Donald really wanted to show her the gorge. He didn't know why, but it had a particular fascination for him.

81

'Come on, the paths are marked and it's on the way back.'

'But that isn't a path.'

'No, but there's one down here somewhere.'

She scrambled down the first bit of the slope until they came to steps leading to what Donald was relieved to find was a marked path.

It was quite dark now and with even the markers hard to see Donald was beginning to wish he had taken Susan's advice and gone back.

'I think it's this way,' he muttered.

'You THINK?'

'Well, I'm pretty sure. I've only been here once.'

'Back. Now.'

Oh dear, her good mood was coming to an end.

'Yes, but I'm not sure which way is back.'

Suddenly there was a crack from the darkness, like a twig being broken underfoot.

'What was that?!' said Susan, eyes wide.

'Oh, maybe a badger.'

'Get us out of here!'

'Ah, I recognise those chestnut trees. They are very old, reputed to have –'

'I don't want a history lesson, just get us out.'

'Yes, what I meant is that if we go along here and then left over the bridge we are almost out.'

There was another crack and what sounded like a moan. Donald felt the hairs standing up on the back of his neck.

'Come on then.' He hurried forward, holding his wife by the hand. She was gripping his very tightly, he noticed.

To his relief the bridge appeared and they turned to go over it.

'This is Ellen Willmott's alpine garden,' he said. 'Or was.'

Another crack.

'Someone's following us!' cried Susan.

'No, there's no-one else here.'

'There is, I tell you. I can sense it.'

As they got over the bridge there was a low moan. It sounded like 'Leave my plants alone,' but that could have been their imagination. It was believable enough for them to start running though, despite the risk of tripping over roots. They didn't stop until they were back at the car and had left Warley Place behind.

'Don't you ever do that to me again,' said Susan icily.
The rest of the journey was made in silence.

14

A Thief in Peril trying to steal from Warley Place

Alex straightened up, stretched his back and sat for a moment on one of the large rocks by the alpine garden. It had been a good day, gardening for once instead of bricklaying or pointing. Rather basic gardening, to be sure, but working with plants nevertheless. He had pulled out weeds when he was sure that is what they were, got rid of the nettles that encroached on the paths and even did a bit of dead-heading and collecting of seeds from plants that Jacob indicated. The weather was good too with a few hours of daylight left. Jacob had said he had some business to attend to at his house so Alex decided to find him and ask what he should do next.

Getting to his feet, he took a short cut through the bushes towards the driveway, but before he got there he stopped. A horse and cart had pulled up outside South Lodge and Jacob was loading boxes of plants on to it. Although seeds were sold and posted to their buyers, plants were not often disposed of in this way. Some were sent to Kew Gardens and other worthy organisations or noted private individuals, but not peddled on the street corner. Even if they were, it would normally be done at the house, not at the gate like this.

He was further puzzled when the tall figure of James Robinson appeared from Jacob's house and the driver of the cart counted out what appeared to be money which he handed over to the butler.

Alex backed into the bushes and thought for a moment. He could continue on his way to see Jacob and hope that perhaps they would tell him what was going on, but they may think he had been spying on them. Jacob's opinion of him was something he really did not want to jeopardise; better not to provoke a confrontation, he thought. Whatever was happening, if Jacob wanted him to know about it he would tell him. He turned and slowly retraced his steps until he reached the rock he had so recently occupied. Sitting down once again, he rested his chin on his hand to think the matter through.

Both Jacob and Robinson were honest men, he was sure of that. But why sell Ellen Willmott's plants in such an apparently underhand way? He knew they were paid very little for what they did and they may well not have received their wages at all at times, but even if that were true stealing from their employer was unthinkable. There must be some other explanation, but he felt uneasy about tackling Jacob or Robinson to find out what it might be. They would rightly tell him to mind his own business.

For the first time the spectre of the devil in this Garden of Eden rose its ugly head.

'The thinking man!'

Alex looked up as Jacob approached.

'Pardon?'

'Rodin's 'Thinking Man'. You look just like him.'

'Oh, yes, of course.'

'Have you finished then?'

'Yes, I think so.'

He pointed to the packets of seeds and the pile of weeds and nettles.

'I wasn't sure which weeds to put on the compost heap and which to burn.'

'I think we'll burn them,' said Jacob. 'The site by the south pond is probably nearest. I'll help you move them.'

Together they loaded up the wheelbarrow and pushed it down the slope where a pile of brushwood lay waiting to be ignited. They threw the weeds on top.

'Another month and we can light that,' said Jacob. 'Well I'm off home. See you tomorrow bright and early.'

'OK, I'll see you then.'

'Anything the matter?' asked Jacob anxiously.

'No, nothing.'

Jacob frowned and went on his way leaving Alex to return the wheelbarrow to the shed by the house.

Put it out of your mind, he told himself as he walked. Brooding on it won't help. There is a perfectly good explanation and Jacob will tell you in time.

He pushed the barrow back past the summer house, the big Spanish chestnuts and down by the walled garden to the shed; leaning it against the wall he checked that the shed was locked.

'Finished for the day Alex?'

He turned. Once again she had appeared out of nowhere. His immediate thought was how strange it was for someone who loved colour so much to be dressed in such sombre colours, a dark coloured coat covering a dark coloured dress and a dark coloured wide brimmed hat on her head. Despite the voluminous pockets in her coat she still carried a large handbag with her, the long carrying strap over one shoulder.

'Yes, finished for the day. It seems a shame to waste what's left of it; the weather is so good for the time of the year.'

'My feeling also,' she said. 'I am off for a walk. Would you join me?'

'I'd be delighted,' said Alex. 'I sometimes forget that there is so much more here than an alpine garden and a walled garden.'

'Come then. The orchard first, I think.'

She led the way round the back of the house and through the house end of the walled garden stopping only briefly.

'I keep a close eye on this each day,' she explained, before moving on round the corner of the house and passing one of her many greenhouses. Alex noticed how she stared straight ahead, apparently not wanting to see the paint peeling off and the occasional broken pane. He sensed a lightening in her step as they passed through a doorway and crossed the drive.

'I have never been in this part of the garden,' he commented as he opened a squeaky iron gate in a yew hedge.

He followed her through, then stopped in his tracks. What faced him was an area about as large as the walled garden with paths darting all ways. Some ran through arches over which clematis or roses grew, others wriggled their way through rockeries. Trees, he had no idea what they were but assumed they bore fruit since it was an orchard, provided some sort of scale to the scene.

She turned, sensing that he was no longer behind her, and smiled.

'It's beautiful,' he said, moving to catch up with her.

She turned towards the rockery and stumbled. His hand shot out instinctively to steady her, then, once she was safe, he took it away again. While he was aware that good manners required him to offer his arm, he knew quite well how independent she wanted to be – and perhaps more importantly to her, how independent she needed to be seen to be.

'The path is a little rough here,' she said.

'Indeed it is.'

'May I take your arm?'

'It would be my pleasure.'

He warmed more and more to this woman with the prickly reputation each time they met.

'The plants are mostly past their best,' she said.

'But it requires little imagination to see what they must have been like and will be like again next year. They are pretty. Cyclamen, aren't they?'

He was looking at some delicate pink flowers protruding a few inches up from silvery green leaves that looked rather like ivy to him.

'They are indeed. *Cyclamen hederifolium*. The Aubretia looks well too in summer, but we need to take some cuttings soon or it will be too late.'

She indicated what now just looked like green foliage spread over some of the larger rocks.

'Have you done any propagating by taking cuttings?'

'Nor by any other means, as far as I know.'

'Oh yes, I forgot. Well I will show you how later on.'

'Are those crocuses?' he asked, puzzled. 'I thought they bloomed in spring.'

'Most of them do, but some do flower in the autumn. Those are not crocuses however, they are colchicums, *Colchicum autumnale* there but other varieties elsewhere. They are sometimes called autumn crocuses but in fact they are part of the Lily family, whereas crocuses are of the Iris family.'

'How interesting – and confusing! Jacob did explain to me about species, genera, families and so on, but the subject is so vast it's hard to remember everything I have been told. I hope it isn't too frustrating talking to someone who is as ignorant as I am about things botanical.'

'Not at all,' she said. 'I do not judge people on what they have not been taught. If they wish to further their knowledge then I am delighted to be able to pass on what I myself have learned. But the one person I cannot abide is the person who pretends to know what he does not.'

They walked on round the garden, up this path, down that one, until his head was ringing with latin names. It was almost a relief finally to emerge from a gate similar to but further on from the one through which they had entered.

'Come,' she said. 'I will show you some trees and the boating lake.'

As they walked past the north side of the coach house Alex noticed that once again she averted her eyes, this time from cold frames as well as another greenhouse, all showing signs of decay.

'Look,' she said. 'Sycamores are a nuisance, scattering their seeds everywhere like weeds, but this is a fine specimen so I allow it to survive.'

'It certainly is,' agreed Alex. 'It must be a hundred years old.'

'Not quite, about sixty years. It was a sapling when we moved in.'

Suddenly she stopped, took her hand from Alex's arm and put her mouth close to his ear.

'That is a Turkey Oak,' she whispered. 'And beneath it is someone stealing my bulbs.'

He had his back to them and they got within ten feet before he heard their approach and whirled round.

'What are you doing?' snapped Ellen Willmott.

'What's it look like?' sneered the unshaven long haired man standing there with a large trowel in one hand and a bulging bag in the other.

'Stealing,' said Alex stepping forward. 'I have no alternative to hand you in to the police.'

'Think so?' said the thief, quickly putting a hand to his waist and pulling out a long and very sharp looking knife. 'And you, you old bat, I'll have that bag while I'm here. There's money in there, I'll be bound.'

'I'd rather keep the bag,' she said calmly. 'But you can have this.'

Alex froze as she pulled out a small but nevertheless deadly looking pistol.

'Yeah, bet it isn't loaded and if it was you wouldn't know how to use it.'

There was a bang and pieces of bark flew off the oak tree inches from the thief's head. He stood there looking at her, mouth open.

'Now I think we'll make sure you don't produce any little thieves,' she said icily, lowering the gun so that it pointed just above his legs.

'No missus, I'm sorry, I won't come back, honest!' he cried. Alex wondered at first if he was bluffing, but the sight of his trousers turning dark first at the crotch and then down each leg convinced him otherwise.

'Drop the knife,' said Ellen Willmott calmly. The knife dropped to the ground. 'Now go. If I or my staff see you here again you will not get a second chance. I will shoot you. If you are still in my sight ten seconds from now I will also shoot you. Go.'

The man needed no second bidding. He ran as fast as his now soggy trousers would allow him.

'My God!' said Alex. 'You scared the hell out of him.'

'I can't stand thieves,' she said as she put her gun away.

'Do you always carry that?'

'No, but when I am out alone I do. I hadn't realised you would be with me.' She took his arm again. 'Now this is a Caucasian wing-nut tree. Grand, isn't it? I think we have time to go round the boating lake before darkness is upon us.'

They walked on in silence for a while.

'Where are the boats?' asked Alex.

'There is only one I am afraid and that is in the boathouse ahead, used only for clearing weeds now.'

They were climbing up a steep slope and on rounding the corner Alex turned to his companion.

'The sweet chestnuts!' he said as they continued along the now flat path. 'Now I know where I am.'

He looked again at her.

'You are - '

He stopped himself. She had been limping, not surprisingly after such a walk and suffering from arthritis as she was.

'I am what?'

'You are very kind to take the time to show me round.'

'You are a liar!' she cried laughing. 'But you are a kindly liar. You were going to say that I was looking tired and limping, and you would have been right. But you wanted to spare my feelings. So yes, perhaps we could rest a while and watch the sun setting over London.'

She guided him to the summer house, where they sat looking as the low clouds took on a crimson glow. She had released his arm to sit down and on impulse he took her hand in his, resting it on his knee and placing his other hand upon it. He took his hand away quickly as he felt her stiffen.

'I do apologise,' he said contritely. 'I meant nothing by it and am being most discourteous.'

'No, don't be sorry,' she said immediately, reaching across and putting his hand back upon hers. 'It feels most comfortable.'

'I have a strange feeling of having been here before,' Alex said eventually. 'A very pleasant feeling. But I know I never have, so it must have been something similar.'

'Or the remembrance of a previous premonition,' she suggested.

'That too is possible.'

They sat watching the sun go down in that companionable silence that is so rare, neither wanting it to end. Then, seeing her shiver slightly as the temperature dropped, Alex stood.

'Come, I will take you back,' he said. 'This has been an evening to remember.'

'It has indeed,' she agreed.

Alex automatically turned towards the bridge over the gorge, but she shivered again.

'No,' she said. 'Not this evening. I don't want to go over the bridge. We shall go back by the wall.'

15

The Terrace

'I think we'll crack on with the terrace today,' said Ben.

'I'm happy enough chipping away at the wall,' volunteered Donald, wanting to see if there were any more loose bricks worth investigating. The deciphering of the journal had been more difficult than he had anticipated and the lack of spare time meant he had only got about a quarter of the way through. So far it had comprised a summary of the author's early life that was curiously lacking in details sufficient to identify him. A glance at a later part of the journal seemed more interesting however and Donald was itching to get on to it.

It was strange that before he retired he had envisaged waking up each morning wondering what he should do that day when in fact he seemed busier than when he was in a full time job!

'No, that can wait. I'd like to make sure we get this finished before the winter. You can help Martin. I'll show you what to do.'

Trying not to show his disappointment Donald followed Ben along the outside of the walled garden to the terrace past the western edge. They climbed down past the 'Danger' notice and stood at the foot of the main terrace retaining wall. It had been dismantled brick by brick, the earth behind it cut back and was in the process of being rebuilt. The steps down from the upper level had not yet been touched and gave some indication of the poor state the whole construction had been in prior to Ben's work being started.

Despite the appearance of being a building site and the obstruction of the view by trees allowed to sprout up since Ellen Willmott's day, the beauty of the spot was even more apparent than it had been at dusk as Donald turned and looked down the slope. He could imagine her and her guests sitting or standing here looking out towards London.

'This is going to be a magical place when you've finished, Ben,' said Donald.

'Er, the wall is this way,' said Ben. 'And it's 'we' not me.'

91

'Well, we're just the helpers,' said someone a few years older and somewhat whiter than Donald, rummaging through a pile of bricks at the other end of the wall. 'It wouldn't happen without you. It's your baby but I'm sure we are all glad to be working on it. I'm Martin by the way.'

'I'm Donald.'

'No, it really is a team effort,' repeated Ben. 'Right, we'll get a full course of bricks on before tea-break.' He pulled a string tight across the top of the bricks to show the line. 'We've got most of the old bricks over there, but some have been broken. Put the best edge facing outwards.'

'Ben,' interrupted Donald. 'I've never laid a brick in my life. Well, not quite true, I did have a go at a coal bunker once but it looked awful when I'd finished.'

'I don't think anyone here had laid bricks before they arrived; now they can all do a passable job. The main thing is to get the mortar right. We use one tin of cement, one of lime, six of sand and this tin here three-quarters full of water. Then all you've got to do is keep the bricks level. And vertical, naturally.'

'Naturally,' agreed Donald, wondering what he had let himself in for.

Donald grabbed a shovel as Ben poured the dry mixture on a big board laying on the ground and together they mixed it thoroughly. Ben fashioned it into a doughnut shape and poured water in the middle. Soon the mixture had been transformed into a sloppy mix.

'Now the tricky bit I suppose,' said Donald nervously.

'Not that tricky, not for our purposes anyway,' grinned Ben, wiping mortar over one surface of a brick and plonking it down on top of the previously laid course. After checking its alignment against the string he wiped the excess mortar off with his trowel, retrieved another brick from a pile and did the same again. Then picking up a wooden block the thickness of a brick and its mortar and putting it down a yard away put a spirit level across the gap. The bubble was right in the middle. He laid a few more before turning to Donald.

'You carry on from where I've left off, check the alignment and the level as I did and you and Martin should meet in the middle,' he said.

'But what if it isn't a full brick width when we meet?'

'It won't be far off if you match the bricks beneath, bridging the joins.'

Donald somewhat tentatively picked up a brick, turned it sideways, scooped up some mortar and wiped it over the end. He turned the brick the right way up – and the mortar all fell off. He hoped Ben hadn't noticed, but turned round to see him grinning from ear to ear.

'Slap it on hard,' he said. 'Then when you turn it over put it straight down where you want it. If you stand and admire it you'll end up with mortar up to your ankles. Right, I'm off to the walled garden. Call if you want me.'

It was slow going but Donald more or less got the hang of it after laying a dozen or so bricks and wasting several trowel-loads of mortar. He was a bit embarrassed at seeing that Martin had laid about twice as many, but with the good start Ben had given him they had almost met in the middle and the mix had been used up.

'How's it going?'

Donald jumped; he hadn't heard Ben arrive.

'Well it's a lot more difficult than it looks when you do it,' he said.

'Not too bad for a new boy,' he said. 'It takes some getting used to, but in a week or two you'll be an old hand.'

He looked at his watch.

'Tea break I think,' he said, pulling a whistle out of his pocket and blowing something that sounded like a steam train whistle.

They grabbed their bags and wandered back to the display area, where several others had already congregated.

As Donald pulled out a bottle of water he was relieved to see Gordon wander in carrying a bundle of drain rods.

'What on earth have you been doing?' asked Martin.

'Looking for Drainiums,' said Gordon.

Martin slung an apple core at him.

'What are Drainiums?' asked Norman. 'Do they look like Geraniums?'

One by one, the odd apple or sandwich consumed, the volunteers wandered back to their jobs. Donald followed Martin back to the terrace to prepare a new mix of mortar for the rest of the morning's work.

'Just fill that tin up with lime,' Ben suggested as Martin dragged a sack of sand to the big mixing board by the wall.

Donald got the little shovel and scooped out the white powder until the tin was full.

'Now pour it on the sand and mix it in.'

Ben stood a little way away, watching as Donald tipped the tin out. The next minute he was coughing and spluttering as a huge cloud of white dust rose from the board.

'I forgot to say, be careful, it's very light,' grinned Ben.

Donald shook his head sorrowfully.

'Now the cement,' said Ben. 'Don't worry, it's not as bad as the lime but you still need to be a bit careful.'

Martin meanwhile had filled a tin with water and a small measure of plasticizer, something that apparently made the mortar easier to work with. Donald had the spade and shovelled at the mixture as Martin added the water.

'I think it's dry enough for cleaning off,' Ben said as he examined the bricks laid before tea. Donald stood back while Martin took a very worn looking wooden tool from Ben and after rubbing a clean line of pointing brushed the loose mortar off the bricks.

'OK, see you later,' said Ben, disappearing back up the slope to the walled garden.

Martin and Donald were soon at work at opposite ends of the wall, each concentrating on keeping the bricks in line, continually with the big spirit level.

'If we were any good at this,' laughed Martin eventually, 'we would be chatting away nineteen to the dozen.'

'Well yours look all right,' said Donald, looking across. 'One or two of mine look a bit wonky.'

'Well it adds to the character of the wall.'

They worked away in silence until after about an hour and a half Martin put down his trowel.

'Well that's the last of the mix,' he said.

'Oh dear, what a shame,' replied Donald in mock sorrow as he scraped up the last of his own mortar to finish pointing the brick he had just laid. 'We haven't quite met in the middle yet, so what happens now?'

'We do it next week. No point in another mix now.'

They washed their tools in a bucket of water and swept the board.

'What about the pointing?'

'We leave that until after lunch. It'll be dry enough then to finish off. Ben likes to be there when we do that – it's important to leave it looking right and he's really good at that. Right, lunch I think.'

Several of the others were already sitting down when they reached the display area but Donald found a space and after brushing the woodworm dust off the sawn log bench seat eased his now aching back as he settled down and opened his rucksack.

'Good grief bricklaying is harder than it looks,' he commented.

'Never mind, we'll get you on something else next week,' consoled Ben, grinning from ear to ear.

'You certainly will when you see my bricks,' said Donald.

'I'll swap clearing the pond for bricklaying!' said a weary-looking Ian.

'Pulling nettles is really easy,' said Steve, rubbing his back. 'I'd swap with me if I were you.'

'They only come here to moan,' explained Ben.

'What do you think of it all then?' asked Frank.

'Well I've only seen the walled garden and the terrace. Oh, and Ben showed me the gorge last time.'

'I didn't realise,' said Martin. 'I'll sort out the pointing and clear up. You have a wander round.'

'I'll show you if you like,' offered Gordon, who had been pulling and cutting sycamores. 'I've finished for the day.'

Donald joined in the small talk while finishing his sandwiches, but his mind was on other things and he was itching to explore the rest of the garden.

The conservatory, right next to where they were sitting, had a certain atmosphere about it when you imagined Ellen Willmott sitting there doing her paperwork or chatting with visitors while looking out at the garden. Although the walls were more or less standing there were no windows or doors; there was no roof and the floor was looking very sorry for itself.

The cellar, now just a big fern-filled hole in the ground, was also a reminder of things as they used to be.

The drive was fascinating, especially when they told him about the pilgrims walking along it long ago.

The terrace would be marvellous when it was restored.

But interesting though all these things were, they didn't have the magic for him that the walled garden and the alpine garden did. Also Jacob Maurer's old cottage had an air of nostalgic mystery about it. He hoped to find more in the garden that would perhaps help him in the deciphering of the journal.

'Coming then Donald?' asked Gordon, standing making for the door – or rather the opening where a door might have been at one time.

'Thanks Martin,' Donald said as he got to his feet, feeling slightly guilty about leaving the clearing up to his colleague.

Gordon led the way through some bushes back to the turning circle at the front of the old house.

'This used to go right through to the north lodge,' he explained as they walked. 'And this building is what's left of what they called the new coach house. It's pretty old, eighteen eighty-two, but it was new as far as Ellen Willmott was concerned. It had a clocktower – a bit grand for a building like that.'

They turned off the old drive and for the next hour Donald was bombarded with details of the rockery, the orchard garden, the beautiful Tree of Heaven, a stunning turkey oak and a Caucasian wing-nut tree, the daffodil bank, the north pond, the boating lake, greenhouses long since gone, enormous cold frames the same. He tried to imagine how Ellen Willmott and her staff could possibly have kept an eye on all that and gave up.

'Right, I'm off now,' said Gordon. You've already seen the walled garden and the terrace. If you're coming too we can go past the gorge.'

They collected their rucksacks from the display area and Gordon led the way along a path to the Spanish chestnuts that he had seen previously with Ben.

'What's that building?' asked Donald as they passed a small brick enclosure with a leaf mould container up against one wall.

'That's the old summer house,' said Gordon. 'Must have been quite a view in the old days.'

They walked on, trees to both sides the names of most of which neither of them had any idea.

'Which one is the persian ironwood Tree?' asked Donald, looking at a notice by the path.

'Come on, it's worth a closer look,' said Gordon, pushing his way through the undergrowth towards what from the path seemed to be a fairly ordinary, if rather untidy, tree. 'Look, see how the branches have fused together?'

Sure enough, everywhere the branches crossed and touched each other they had formed a fused junction covered with bark.

'Quite often people who plant them keep them pruned,' explained Gordon. 'Then they never see this effect.'

'It's fascinating.'

'It marks the beginning of what was the alpine garden,' said Gordon. 'You can see from the large rocks that have started to appear and the valley beginning to deepen.'

'Ben showed me this last week,' said Donald, 'but he was on his way to the store so we didn't stay long.'

Then suddenly there it was again. The old alpine garden, but with none of the original plants apparent at all. Donald felt a strange feeling down the back of his neck.

'What's that?' he said, pointing to what looked like the remnants of a couple of stone arches over the gorge, with some rusty metal girders. 'Presumably the site of a bridge at some time.'

'No, that was the roof of her filmy fern cave. She had some ferns that needed special conditions so she built it for them. Doors at both ends – you can see the remains of one of them – and thick glass over the top. We don't know how she got water in there, because it seems to be slightly higher than the level of the stream and anyway there is no outlet. The south pond is just past it though, so it's possible just enough water got through to keep it moist.'

'It really is fantastic. All these rocks! I just can't believe it.'

'We haven't got time now,' said Gordon. 'Or I haven't. But if you go on a bit there's a bird hide. You can sit there, or even go round it down to the pond – but best have someone with you in case you slip.'

'Magic,' breathed Donald. 'Pure magic.'

16

Alex's Case is subject to Review

Ellen Willmott stuck a small red-topped stick in the ground and kneeled down to examine the plant. It was pretty obvious the poor *Gentiana bavarica* needed water – the little rill had almost dried up. Why did she always have to let her gardeners know like this? They had eyes in their heads, didn't they? Such a lovely flower too, with its iridescent blue flowers.

She lifted her head as she heard a car crunching on the gravel at the house, followed by the slamming of car doors. There was the murmur of voices as they spoke to Robinson. She turned her attention to *Daphne cneorum* but it was well past its best. Just a few pink flowers and leaf spot just starting to appear. She heard footsteps approaching and turned her attention back to the much better looking *Gentiana*. There was a cough from behind her.

'Doctor Townsend,' she said as she got to her feet. 'How nice to see you again.'

'This is Captain Perkins,' said the doctor. 'The officer I mentioned on the telephone. He's reviewing Alex's case and would like to have a chat with him, if that's all right with you?'

Captain Perkins stuck out his hand which, with a perceptible hesitation, Ellen Willmott shook. She had somehow expected a short plump man with a moustache and small hard eyes, but in fact although he was quite short, he was rather thin and his eyes were big and bulging rather than small. He did have a moustache, but it looked incongruous on such a narrow face. He was probably in his forties, fifty maybe. Old enough to have escaped being sent to France.

'And what is the purpose of your review?' she asked.

'I am afraid that is military business,' he said, while to her amusement he discreetly searched for something on which to wipe his now dirty hand. She handed him a grubby rag from her apron pocket which he took with thanks and returned to her after a perfunctory wipe, probably wondering if he was adding to or diminishing the numbers of bacteria present on his hand.

'That may be, but the war is over and Alex is my responsibility at the moment. What do you want to discuss with him?'

'We need to know what happened in France to make him lose his memory. If he has lost his memory, that is.'

Stephen Townsend's eyes rolled up into his head.

'What do you mean by *if* he has lost his memory?' said Ellen Willmott through tight lips, the words coming out individually like bullets from a gun.

'Now look here madam,' said Captain Perkins. 'You know nothing about military matters, I do. You know nothing about medical matters, Townsend here does. So please just let us get on with our jobs, there's a good woman.'

Stephen Townsend groaned.

'I am well enough acquainted with military matters to know that millions of good young men have been killed while their so-called betters were safely tucked away well behind the lines making silly decisions about how many of those lives could be sacrificed today and how many tomorrow. I am well enough acquainted with medical matters to know that Alex certainly has lost his memory and it seems to originate with some very traumatic experience he suffered while fighting the enemy.'

'Fighting the enemy, or running away from it?'

Ellen Willmott's eyes flashed. 'Rubbish. Anyone with half a mind can see he's no coward.'

'You're very protective towards him. Is anything going on that we should know about?'

'How dare you. Get off my land. Now.'

'Afraid I can't do that old girl.'

Stephen Townsend held his hand up.

'Please Ellen, can I speak?'

She nodded, furious with herself for allowing matters to get this far.

He took his colleague aside. 'Captain,' he whispered, but loud enough for Ellen Willmott to hear. 'Miss Willmott has powerful friends. Among them Queen Alexandra and Queen Mary. She is on particularly good terms with the latter, who visits her here, and well enough known to the former to dedicate her book, *The Genus Rosa*, to her. I could also list her other very influential friends but it would take an hour at least. If you value your career I would suggest you give her the respect she not only wants, but also deserves.'

Ellen Willmott was amused to see the Captain's Adam's apple going up and down and his tongue licking his now dry lips. After taking a deep breath he turned to her.

'I do apologise madam. I seem to have got off to a very unfortunate start. I would be most grateful if we could begin again.'

Stephen Townsend mouthed a 'please' at her, but she was still tempted to send him packing. The problem was that she did not really know what harm it might do to Alex if she gave way to her natural inclination.

'Very well,' she said, unable to stop herself making it sound as condescending as she could. 'But I have one condition. I should like to be present. If Alex wishes it, that is. If any military matters of a confidential nature are discussed then I shall withdraw.'

'Thank you madam, that would be quite in order,' said a relieved captain.

'Come this way then, we shall find him by the summer house. He should be repairing the brickwork there so we can talk with him with minimum interruption to his work.'

'*Delphinium* 'Miss Willmott',' she said pointing to a flower as they walked.

'It's doing well,' said the doctor.

The captain grunted, obviously not interested in flowers. She wondered if he would admit to it.

'Are you familiar with this one?' she asked him. 'It's *Desfontainia spinosa.*'

'Yes, of course.'

It did look beautiful, five foot high with myriads of red and yellow flowers.

'And what do you think of the *Daphne alpina*?' she asked, looking at a small plant with red flowers. He glanced at it and said it was pleasant enough, which it was, except that it was a *Dianthus microlepis*. She amused herself by making up fictitious names for a few plants before getting bored and they completed the walk to the summer house in silence.

'Just sit there for a moment if you will,' she said as they reached the little brick building. Little more than a hut, it had circular windows on each side and a solid back, but the front opened out to a view of London almost twenty miles away through a row of Spanish chestnut trees. 'Alex does not appear to be here. He is probably helping Jacob.'

She started to walk off, then sniffed the air. She recognised the unmistakeable aroma of cigarette smoke. Walking smartly to the Spanish chestnut trees she strode round the huge trunk of the oldest of the seven and dragged a youth out.

'Right Michael, boating lake weeds, now.'

'But Miss Willmott,' he protested.

'Now. And if I see you smoking in the boat you'll do it tomorrow too,' she called as he walked off.

She turned to make her way to the alpine garden just in time to see the captain putting a pipe back in his pocket.

'Lovely view of London from here,' she said. 'Today is particularly clear, but often in winter it is shrouded in a yellow smoke. How people breathe in it I cannot imagine. Some people, like young Barnaby there, actually like it and carry their portable smoke generators with them. Disgusting habit.'

The captain nodded.

'Alex?' she called, as she walked away smiling to herself. 'Captain Perkins is here.'

Alex came scrambling out of the gorge just a hundred yards away.

'No need to hurry,' she said. 'Do him good to wait. If you want him to go just give me the nod and he'll be gone before you know it. What's that?'

She pointed to an orchid at least two feet high with rosy-purple blossoms.

'That is *Orchis foliosa*, from Madeira,' he said.

'Jacob teaches you well and you learn fast.' She was impressed. 'Oh well, I suppose we should find out what he wants to know.'

They walked the short distance to the summer house in silence, each deep in thought.

'Hello again Alex,' said the doctor. 'This is Captain Perkins. He has come to ask you some questions to perhaps enable us to piece together what exactly happened in France and who you really are.'

'Good morning captain,' said Alex.

'Good morning Alex. But since you are strictly speaking still in military service I think it would be better if you called me 'sir', don't you?'

'If you wish,' said Alex reluctantly.

'May I speak?' said Ellen Willmott. Then without waiting for an answer she continued. 'From what I have seen Alex is certainly an officer and quite possibly one of superior rank to yourself captain. His natural tendency to call you by your rank suggests that too. I wonder if it would be better for him to continue respectfully to address you in that way?'

'Well...'

'And also, if he is still in military service, may I ask how much he is being paid?'

She noticed a spot of blood appearing on the captain's lip and his cheeks colouring somewhat.

'If all turns out well and he regains his memory his back pay will be given to him. At the moment without knowing his rank we don't know how much that should be. However if it means so much to you he may continue to call me by my rank.'

'Thank you captain,' said Alex. 'Now how may I help?'

'Well as a start you could tell me what you do remember.'

'Very little I am afraid. I must have been a pilot because when I see an aeroplane pass overhead I get a great feeling of remorse. No fear exactly, although there is some of that. Mostly remorse.'

'Remorse? What about?'

'I really don't remember. I remember being found in a German prisoner of war camp and brought back to England and everything from then on, but before that point everything is blank.'

'Even your name?'

'Even my name,' confirmed Alex.

'What about hobbies? What do you do in your spare time?'

'I spend most of my time in the garden. I like it. I must have been musical at one time because I played the piano for Miss Willmott on one occasion.'

'Ah! So you remembered how to play the piano? Then you do remember things from before you went to France?'

'Not consciously, no.'

'Excuse me captain,' broke in Doctor Townsend. 'This is absolutely typical of memory loss brought about by a traumatic experience. The patient's autobiographical knowledge is forgotten

102

but skills learned are not. So if Alex were to say he had forgotten how to play the piano I would be suspicious. He could ride a bicycle. He might even be able to fly an aeroplane, although if the traumatic experience was associated with flying then who knows what might happen.'

'Why can he remember one and not the other?'

'I can see you don't believe me captain, but the mysteries of the brain are a long way from being understood. Please just accept what I say as a fact, but not one that can be fully explained.'

'Very well,' grunted Captain Perkins. 'Will he ever remember what happened?'

'I hope so.'

'What do you think Alex?'

'I really don't know captain. I think so, because every so often something triggers off glimmerings of memory. As I have already said, when an aeroplane comes close I feel as though.... well it's the same feeling as having a word on the tip of your tongue. You feel it's there but you don't know how to retrieve it.'

'Do you want to retrieve it?' asked Dr Townsend.

'Yes. But I am also frightened of what will happen then.'

Captain Perkins sniffed.

'Captain, you have no idea of what Alex may have been through,' said Ellen Willmott. 'So a sniff like that is most uncalled for.'

'Now listen here,' he started to retort.

Dr Townsend gave a little cough.

'Just clearing my nose. Must be all this pollen. Hayfever. Sorry.'

'Is there anything else we can help you with?' asked Ellen Willmott.

'I don't think so, is there captain?' said the doctor.

'No, I suppose not.'

Ellen Willmott turned to Alex. 'Thank you then Alex. I expect Jacob could do with your help.'

'So what do you think Stephen?' she asked the doctor. 'How long before he does regain his memory?'

'It's not possible to say. Something may trigger it. We could try taking him to an aerodrome and sitting him in an aeroplane, but that might do more harm than good. As a last resort, maybe. His brain is more likely to recover in an atmosphere like this. If you don't mind him staying longer it is my opinion that that would give him the best chance.'

'No, I don't mind at all. In fact we enjoy having him.'

'Captain?' prompted the doctor.

'Yes, I think I could go along with that. Review in another month?'

'Yes, another month. But meanwhile I will keep a closer eye on him here and Ellen will certainly contact me if anything interesting should happen. I know the way back,' the doctor continued to Ellen Willmott. 'Don't let us disturb you any longer.'

They turned and walked back through the trees towards the house and she heard the captain's faint voice.

'God she scares me more than the Hun. Don't know that I want to come back here.'

'Good,' she murmured. Mission accomplished.

17

A Problem

Donald put the page marker in the Journal and closed it, rubbing his eyes.

'Have you found out who he was yet?' his wife asked, looking up from her own book.

'No. Not his name, anyway. I've tried the internet, the library and the Essex Record Office. It's a complete blank. I've started to wonder whether it's a hoax of some sort.'

'It's a bit elaborate for a hoax. No-one could have known that you would find that loose brick, and it's obviously very old. It'll probably be cleared up by the end.'

'Well it's certainly interesting reading about him and it's getting easier to fill in the damaged bits.'

'Perhaps they'll know about him at Warley Place?'

'I doubt it, but I'll ask when I've finished going through it. Whenever that will be – it's taking far longer than I thought it would.'

'My goodness, is that the time? I'd better get some dinner on,' said his wife, putting her book down and getting quickly to her feet.

''Fancy going out tonight instead?'

Her face lit up.

'That would be nice. Can we afford it?'

'Yes, it's not that expensive. We could always practice eating haggis.'

A slight chill passed through the air. Shut up Don, he thought. Things had been so much better recently.

'It's a bit late to go far, would Wang Pau's be OK?'

She nodded. 'Fine with me.'

After carefully putting the journal away he joined her in the bedroom and watched her doing her hair. She was certainly good looking for someone in her mid fifties, he thought to himself. Looking at him in the mirror, she smiled, and slightly embarrassed he turned away and opened the wardrobe door.

There, neatly lined up on hangers, was a row of sparkling clean beautifully ironed shirts, several suits, a light coloured sports jacket and a dark blazer.

I really am looked after, he thought. I don't have to think about washing or ironing, my suits got taken to the cleaners regularly when I was working, I get my meals cooked, the house is always clean and tidy, and the garden is a picture. All I do is moan about being bored and having to take her mother to Spain on holiday every year.

'Which one do you think?' he asked.

'Whatever you like, but the blazer would look nice,' she said from behind him.

'Yes dear,' he said automatically, putting the one back and taking out the other. 'Which tie do you think?'

She came up behind him, putting her arms round his waist.

'I don't care which tie you wear, or whether you wear one at all,' she said.

'Oh yes, I'm supposed to be decisive, aren't I,' he joked, opting for a safe striped one and smiling at the puzzled frown he saw on his wife's face in the mirror.

'I'm looking forward to this,' she said as the front door shut behind them and they stepped out into the warm evening.

He reached in his pocket for the car keys.

'Let's walk, it's not far,' she said slipping her hand in his.

They walked in companionable silence until they reached the High Street.

'What are you smiling at?' she asked.

'Me, a month ago, walking up here to get the paper and going back without it,' he said shaking his head. 'I don't know what came over me.'

He didn't tell her about stepping out in front of the car.

'Table for two?' he asked the Chinese manager as the door closed behind them. I wonder if he really is Chinese, he thought, or a European made up to look like one.

With a sick feeling he realised he should have booked. The manager was sucking his teeth looking for an empty table.

'For you, of course.'

Relief swept over him.

They were led round the corner to a table in front of the window to the street.

106

'Is this table suitable? Some people like being able to see out while they are eating.'

'This is fine,' he said.

Interesting, he thought as they settled themselves into their chairs, how she makes all the decisions at home, but is happy for me to make them when we are out.

They stared at the menu.

'Set meal, or do you want to try something different?'

'Meal 'B' looks nice,' she said.

The waiter smiled his agreement and took the menus.

'A drink sir?'

'Yes please. Dear? Amontillado? Fine, and one for me too. Thanks.'

Life's not really that bad, he thought to himself as they sat waiting for their drinks. I have a wife I can take anywhere, a nice house, a little car, and we can afford to go out like this occasionally. Many couldn't.

'Should you be drinking alcohol with your pills,' she whispered.

'I suppose not,' he said, 'if I was still taking them. I keep forgetting though. In fact I think I feel better if I don't.'

The waiter broke him off from his musings with the drinks. He saw his wife looking at him, a quiet smile on her face. She hadn't smiled very often recently, not with feeling, but when she did it was nice.

'A penny for them?' she asked.

He smiled back, realising that in fact he already had been half smiling to himself.

'Just thinking how nice it is to do this,' he said. 'And how nice you looked.'

'Thank you.'

He thought for a moment.

'Sue,' he said, a little furrow appearing on his brow.

'Yes?' she smiled, a little puzzled at his sudden seriousness.

'I really am sorry about Scotland. I thought I was doing the right thing. I got carried away by Gordon and the brochures. I should have discussed it with you first. It was stupid of me.'

'No, forget it. I shouldn't have reacted the way I did in the first place. I think we've both got to learn that being positive and decisive isn't the same as organising something that involves both of us without discussing it first.'

107

She stopped as the waiter brought the soups to their table.

'This is delicious,' he said. 'One day we'll have to try something more exotic, rather than the set dishes. Trouble is I don't know what half the other things are.'

'Me neither, but I'm sure they will help us out.'

'That's our first joint decision then,' he grinned. 'We'll ask them what we should have. I'm not sure if that's being decisive or not!'

He hadn't felt this relaxed for a very long while. He had a feeling he was going to enjoy his retirement after all.

'I feel a bit of a simpleton at Warley,' he said. 'I love it there but I haven't a clue about the plants.'

'Well it's certainly made a difference to you,' she agreed. 'You've never been more relaxed. And you'll pick the plant names up as time goes by. Mind you, the washing machine is likely to become a solid mass of concrete with the mortar dust you bring home on your clothes!'

'Ah, yes. I must get some overalls. The trouble is it's so hot at the moment.'

'I was only joking, it's not a problem.'

The rest of the meal passed pleasantly and suddenly Donald was disappointed to realise it was time to go.

'Funny how impromptu outings, even only to the local Chinese restaurant, can be so pleasant,' he said as they left for home.

'I've had a lovely evening,' she agreed, taking his hand.

Several minutes later they were home.

'I'm tired,' he said. 'It's been a good day though.'

'Yes,' she agreed. 'A good day.'

He took his shoes and jacket off and sat deep in thought, not aware of her eyes on him.

'I'm off to bed,' she said. 'Coming?'

'Yes. I'll be up in a minute.'

He reached for the Journal while she was in the bathroom, pulled out the page marker and started to read, then put it down. Now wasn't the time to get engrossed.

He really ought to learn more about plants; the ones at Warley, anyway. There was a specialist group that walked round Warley Place on the last Tuesday of each month who didn't get involved in refurbishment but did keep an eye on all things botanical. Perhaps he could join them. He reached for his wife's diary to check on which day the last Tuesday fell and froze. There, for Monday morning, was an appointment.

'Ted, 10.30' was all it said.

Oh God no! Not Sue. Not seeing someone while he was at Warley.

Suddenly his world was shattered.

He walked slowly upstairs, changed into his pyjamas and cleaned his teeth.

'Donald,' she said as he climbed into bed. 'There's something I really must tell you.'

Oh no, not now. He needed time to show her how good they were together, what a good life they would have.

'No, it's OK, I know we said we should discuss everything but – '

'Donald, I want to. It was going to be a secret, but you really ought to know.'

'But – '

'I'm having driving lessons?'

'You're what?'

'I'm having driving lessons. Ted, down the road, is teaching me. Mum said she'd pay but I should have talked to you about it first. I wanted it to be a surprise though, so I've been having them while you are at Warley Place.'

'That's brilliant,' he said. 'You'll pass without too much trouble, then when you are driving I can tell you to mind that bus and - '

He was cut short by a poke in the ribs.

'You really don't mind?'

'I really don't mind. You don't know how pleased I am.'

18

Alex is Reassured about the Sale of Plants

'I think we will do a bit of concreting today,' said Jacob as Alex joined him by the shed.

'What about my botanical lesson?' asked Alex.

Jacob had taken to giving him a short lesson each day on one aspect or another of the plants in the garden - the derivation of their names, where they came from, what they needed to survive, and so on. But not too much at any one time, Jacob had insisted. Otherwise it would be confusing. It was like introducing him to a group of people and expecting him to remember all their names when all that would happen is that he wouldn't remember any. But one at a time, that was different.

'We can discuss something while we are working,' said Jacob. 'Or rather while we start working. I'll leave you to it once you know what to do and you can think about what I have said and ask me questions later on.'

'That's fine with me,' said Alex. 'What are we concreting?'

'The walnut tree.'

'The what?!'

Just at that moment a small tousle haired boy came running up to them. He was a smaller version of Jacob, without the moustache and the flat cap.

'Dad, the man has come for the plants,' he gasped, bending over with a hand on each knee while he recovered his breath.

'Alex, this is Max, my eldest,' explained Jacob. He turned back to the boy. 'Tell them we'll be right along,' he said. 'But no need to run so fast, take your time.'

The boy turned and started to walk back to South Lodge, but couldn't contain himself and was soon running as fast as he had before.

Jacob, who had been watching him, turned to Alex.

'Such energy!' he said. 'He makes me feel so old!'

He looked towards the big house and frowned.

'I don't know where James is,' he said. 'I wonder if you would come and help.'

'Help what?'

'No need to look so alarmed, we're not selling off Miss Willmott's plants. Not really.'

He started walking towards his home, Alex at his side.

'You are aware of her financial situation?'

'Well, broadly speaking yes,' said Alex. 'I don't know the details and don't want to, but I am aware that the estate is struggling to make ends meet.'

'That's putting it mildly,' said Jacob. 'Her sister Rose has offered to help, but you know Ellen Willmott.'

'Oh yes, I can see the problem.'

'Well Rose is concerned that some of the rare plants that Miss Willmott has taken so much trouble to find and to grow will soon be gone. I think she is right, we just haven't the time or money to keep them all going. So I propagate what I can in my own back garden or when she is away even take some from her own beds, and Rose takes them to ensure their survival. She pays handsomely for them.'

'But what happens to the money? Ellen Willmott is no fool, she will know what the plants are actually worth.'

Jacob smiled.

'Yes, you are right, she would immediately smell a rat, but she doesn't know what is going on. If she does find out, our records are not kept in sufficient detail for her to check, even if she wanted to. That is why always two of us are present when money changes hands. Up to now it has been James and myself, but I think he must be with Miss Willmott so we can't disturb him. He keeps an account of money received and we spend it on the estate as we see fit and in a way that she would approve. We let Rose know how the money was spent.'

'Doesn't she wonder how such things are being paid for?'

'Maybe, but she hasn't questioned anything yet.'

'What loyal employees she has,' said a relieved Alex.

Jacob laughed.

'I'll wager you thought we were stealing plants and pocketing the money,' he said.

111

'No,' protested Alex. 'But I did wonder what was going on and after Ellen shot at the thief stealing her bulbs I feared for your own safety.'

'I have told her that from time to time I would like to sell some of my own produce and she has agreed,' he said. 'So there is little danger. She has always been concerned about the possibility of theft and now if she does miss any that I have removed she will place the blame elsewhere.'

'What a shame it has come to this.'

They reached the little cottage to find that Max and his brothers had already brought most of the boxes of plants to the front gate and they helped Jacob and Alex to load the cart.

'Fifty pounds,' said the driver, handing over an envelope.

Jacob opened it and asked Alex to count it with him.

'Fifty pounds,' he confirmed. 'You will stay for some food?'

'No, thank you. The old girl will see if I stay here, then we'll have some explaining to do. I'll stop for some grub on the way.'

They watched as his horse trotted off towards Brentwood, where the plants would be transferred to the train.

'Right,' said Alex as they walked back up the drive. 'Now what was it we were to be concreting?'

'The walnut tree. Its trunk is going rotten and is already quite hollow so we are going to fill the open bit with concrete and when it is set put a steel band round it. That should stop it falling over for a few years.'

'And where is this tree?'

'Just the other side of the carriageway facing the house.'

Alex sighed.

'Isn't it going to look rather awful?'

'Possibly, but not as awful as if it fell down. We will make the surface as wrinkly as we can and brush some dirt and bark into it when it is nearly dry, then later on cow dung. It will soon weather into the same sort of colour as the tree. It is far enough away from the house not to matter too much – although her majesty will certainly come and make a very close inspection followed by some disparaging remarks and instructions as to how to put it right.'

'What will you do then?'

'Nothing.'

'I beg your pardon?'

'Nothing. Please don't misunderstand me; you know I think the world of her. But to some extent she is living in the past when she had apparently unlimited funds to play with and a small army of staff to obey her every whim. So I let her indulge in her remarks and wishes and off she goes. She plays the game too – she never comes back and complains that I haven't done what she asked to put things right.'

'She certainly is a remarkable woman,' said Alex wistfully. Memories of another woman flashed through his mind. Someone he had known recently but what seemed a lifetime ago.

'Come on then Alex,' said Jacob. 'I'll show you what needs to be done. You can come back for the tools and cement later.'

They walked towards the front of the house, past the walled garden and the lawn.

'My goodness,' said Alex with mock seriousness. 'The *Trifolium repens* is looking well today.'

Jacob smiled. 'You are allowed to use common names sometimes. The word clover would have sufficed.'

'Ah!' said Alex, the corners of his mouth twitching. 'But then I might confuse you because it could be Hare's foot clover, Rough clover, Red clover...'

'And how do you know it isn't any one of those?' Jacob asked.

Alex conceded defeat. 'All right, you win! I found a book in the bothy.'

'I guessed that,' said Jacob. 'You really do like words, don't you? Latin as much as English. Do you know what *Trifolium repens* means?'

'Well I assume 'trifolium' means three leaves, that is obvious. But I must confess 'repens' is more difficult. The only thing I can think of is that it means creeping, because that's what clover does.'

'You are absolutely right.'

They had passed the house by now and were crossing the meadow to the walnut tree, standing lonely looking and not a little sad in the middle of the expanse of grass.

'*Bipedula repens*, I think,' whispered Alex as the sound of wood cracking underfoot came from behind a beech tree some fifty yards away. Sure enough, Ellen Willmott appeared and made her way towards them.

'You two are looking very pleased with yourselves, considering the early hour,' she commented.

'I tried to get one up on Jacob,' explained Alex, 'but came off second best.'

'And that pleases you?' Her brow was creased in puzzlement.

'What always pleases me is learning something new, and I have learned something new already this morning.'

'And what is that?'

'The meaning of *Trifolium repens*, Miss Willmott.'

She turned to Jacob.

'You will get rid of it before the day is out.'

'Yes Miss Willmott,' Jacob groaned.

'I have also learned something else, Miss Willmott,' continued Alex, grinning from ear to ear. 'Not to mention *Trifolium repens* within your earshot.'

Ellen Willmott's eyes opened wide, her hands clenched shut. Then creases appeared at the sides of her mouth and her eyes started to twinkle. In the end she gave in and laughed openly.

'Just don't go too far Alex,' she said.

'I do apologise. It's just that I have been so happy here for the last few weeks, sometimes I say things before I think.'

'You are a breath of fresh air,' she said. 'I mean no disrespect to you Jacob; I could not manage without you. Don't change Alex. But don't make comments like that in front of the men.'

'I wouldn't dream of it.'

She nodded and stood there for a moment as if reluctant to move on.

'The Verbascums are well past their best,' she commented eventually.

Jacob nodded.

'They aren't my favourite flower,' Alex said.

There was silence for a moment and Alex saw Jacob trying unsuccessfully to stifle a smile.

'Have you ever looked at a *Verbascum*?' she asked eventually. 'I mean *really* looked at one?'

'Well, I've seen them as I have walked about the garden.'

She rummaged about in one of her pockets and extracted an eyeglass. Then going over to one of the plants she pulled off one of the little flowers and came back to him, passing him both the flower and the glass.

114

'Look inside the flower,' she said. 'Tell me what you see.'

He did as he was bidden. It was hard to focus at first, but suddenly it all became clear. He adjusted the glass to see different parts more clearly, first the stamens, then the myriads of purple hairs, the veins on the petals themselves. He had no idea how long he had been looking when he realised Ellen Willmott was speaking.

'Well?' she was asking with a smile, for she already knew the answer. 'What do you see?'

'I see another world,' he whispered. 'It's beautiful. I've never looked at a flower in that way before.'

'They are not all as beautiful as that inside,' she said. 'But many are, often the ones that are less stunning on the outside.'

'Thank you,' he said. 'I learn something every day, but today I have learned something really special.'

'I'm glad.'

She turned and walked away.

'You could get away with murder as far as she is concerned,' said Jacob before turning his attention back to the tree. 'Before we do anything else we need to put some shuttering round the trunk to hold the concrete in place while it dries. We'll go up in stages to avoid too much shock to the tree, just a couple of feet initially. Are you all right?'

'I'm not sure,' said Alex slowly. 'When I relax like this I find memories coming back in bits and pieces. Last night Miss Willmott asked me in and we spoke about things.'

'You're honoured! She is always very friendly to her staff – unless they do something wrong! – but doesn't ask them in to her house. Where did you go?'

'To the Library, then to the Music Room.'

'Really? Did she play her violin for you?'

'No. I saw two there, but she didn't play them. I played the piano and she sang.'

Jacob's jaw dropped.

'I started to remember things, and they are coming back to me now. Not much, but enough to frighten me. There is something I don't want to remember, I am sure of it.'

'May I ask what you do remember?'

'Yes, of course. I remember another woman. A beautiful woman who sang the same song that Miss Willmott sang last night. 'The Last Rose of Summer'. I believe we were to be married.'

'But you weren't?'

'No. I think we were waiting until the war was over. The war!' He shuddered. 'I hate killing. Always have.'

'I think most people hate killing. Many of those who survived have been scarred for life by their experience. One has only to visit the asylum to see.'

Alex nodded. 'Yes, I know. But there is something more.'

'Did an aeroplane drop bombs on you, or shoot at you?'

'No... why do you think that?'

'From your reaction when one flies near us here.'

'Oh. Yes, of course. No, I was a pilot.'

He started to shake.

'Jacob, can you imagine what it is like to shoot someone with a machine gun and see what it does to them?'

He felt his throat closing up and his eyes filling with water. He felt Jacob's arm round his shoulders.

'Don't talk about it if you don't want to.'

'I don't remember any more,' he managed to say. 'I don't want to remember any more!'

19

Point and Counterpoint

'So what are we doing today?' asked Donald as they plodded up to the old turning circle where Ben and Frank parked their cars packed full of equipment.

'Bracken,' said Ben. 'Pulling bracken. At least, you are. And Gordon, Norman and Steve. By post six.'

The route for visitors was marked by various direction arrows and numbered posts, the explanatory leaflet referring to the post numbers to tell them about points of interest.

'But what about the wall?'

'Plenty of time for the wall. Carla is having a go at it with Martin, but we need to get the bracken up before it spreads its spores everywhere.'

Donald finished lacing up his boots. He felt a bit envious of Carla and Martin. He saw it as his wall now that he had found the Journal, even though they had been working on it a long time before he came on the scene. It was very unlikely that there was anything else there but one never knew.

'Make sure you leave the ferns. Some of them are rare,' continued Ben.

'How do we tell the difference between ferns and bracken?' asked Gordon.

'Come on, I'll show you,' said Ben, walking the few yards to the edge of the old cellar. It was just a hole in the ground now, with the walls showing through an assortment of plants in places but mostly as obscured as the floor. The building over it had been demolished before the Second World War.

'There,' he said, pointing down into the cellar. 'Those clumps there, they are all ferns.'

'Oh,' said Gordon. 'A fully fern-ished cellar.'

Ben shuddered and ignored him.

'Over there, those things sprouting up singly, not in clumps, they are bracken. Be careful of the foxgloves. Some of the bracken is in with the bamboo. You needn't be careful of the bamboo, but don't bother to pull it up or cut it down, just leave it.

Have a close look at the ferns and you'll see the stems are slightly different too. I promise you, after a few hours of pulling bracken you'll recognise it instantly!'

'What about the nettles?' asked Steve.

'Just concentrate on the bracken, the nettles can wait. If any are in your way just pull them up too, but don't waste too much time on them.'

'What's that tree there?' asked Donald, pointing at a lone tree in a field opposite the turning circle.

'That's an old walnut tree,' said Steve. 'The trunk had been eaten away, or was dying, or something and Ellen Willmott had it filled with concrete so it wouldn't fall down.'

'I thought it looked a bit strange. It's lasted well. Does it still produce walnuts?'

'Oh yes. But the squirrels get them. Ask Frank to show you some time, he knows all about it.'

He grabbed the handles of the barrow and started walking. 'Come on, post six.'

'Susan still kicking up about you coming here?' asked Gordon as he walked alongside Donald.

'Actually no. In fact she seems pleased that I've found something like this. She goes off to her mother's or her mother goes there, I'm not sure which. She's also thinking of taking up an Adult Education Class so it's worked out very well. I can't thank you enough for suggesting it.'

He did not mention the driving lessons. Susan had asked him to keep it a secret in case she failed and he could understand her concern.

'I'm glad,' said Gordon, a puzzled look crossing his face. 'I thought perhaps she might object.'

'No, as I said, she seems to be pleased.'

'So she's not grumpy any more?'

'No, she's not,' said Donald. 'I'm not sure about her mother though. She'd prefer me working on the house.'

'Oh well, imagine you're pulling her hair out when you're pulling bracken,' he said as they came to a stop. Norman came walking up behind them.

'Sorry I'm late lads,' he said. 'Hello, I'm Norman.'

'I'm Donald. I think we met last week..'

'What are we doing then?'

'Pulling bracken, Norman,' said Gordon. 'Bracken is –'

'I know what bracken is,' said Norman.

Donald looked around and groaned. An area about thirty metres long stretching back about twenty metres on both sides of the path was packed with bracken about a metre high; and nettles, and bamboo reaching above his head. He pulled his gardening gloves on, joined the other two, bent down and started to pull.

'Throw them on the path,' said Steve. 'Then we'll take them to the bonfire site later.'

Thank goodness Susan was happy with what he was doing. She'd been very impatient with him at times. Could it have been partly his fault? Was he that bad? The pills the doctor gave him had helped a bit but made him a bit drowsy so although it helped him put up with her it seemed to increase her irritation with him. Actually now he came to think about it he'd forgotten to take his pill again this morning and didn't seem any the worse for it.

He lost track of time. Pull, throw, pull, throw.

When did they start, well, getting irritable with each other? They'd lived reasonably happily for years. She hadn't minded working too while they were buying their home. They could have afforded that on his salary, but not the car and the holidays. They were good, the holidays. Well, OK. She seemed to enjoy them more than him. Shame they hadn't had any children, but by the time they could afford it it was too late.

Pull, throw, pull, throw.

Perhaps that was the underlying problem now. She was bored. She needed a bit of excitement, and although he had the time to try to help now he had retired and was at home more, Donald was honest enough with himself to know that he wasn't a particularly exciting sort of person. This was what he wanted, peace and quiet pulling bracken. He had to admit, though, that she had been a bit better lately. In fact good company most of the time.

Pull, throw, pull, throw – he suddenly heard a whistle.

'Thank God, tea break,' said Steve. 'We might as well stay here and sit in the sun rather than go to the display area.'

Donald rubbed his back as he straightened and made his way to a bench by the path, where they all sat down. He could hardly believe that an hour and a half had passed.

'I know what I was going to ask,' said Donald to Steve as he pulled an apple from his bag. 'I was discussing Leylandii the other day and had a disagreement about how to pronounce the ending. Am I right, is it 'ee eye'?

'ee eye,' confirmed Steve.

'Oh,' muttered Gordon.

'The ii means 'named after' in botanical terms. So something called Smithii would be named after someone called Smith.'

'So there is likely to be a plant called 'Willmottii?'

'Ah, no, it's not that simple,' said Steve. 'I believe there are some called Willmottiae though. The 'ae' at the end is the feminine gender, 'ii' is masculine.'

'So –'

'No good asking me anything else,' said Steve. 'I think I just exhausted my knowledge of plant names. It all seems horribly complicated but I'm sure it's easy if you really understand it.'

'The only name I know is *Brackonium willmottiae*,' said Gordon.

'What's that?' asked Donald.

'It's a special hybrid combining the hardiness of bracken and the simple beauty of the fern. Ben was telling us about it earlier. Unfortunately the hardiness didn't take too well and this is the only place where they have survived. There are no others in the entire country. There are a couple over there.'

He waved his hand towards a particularly barren part of the ground.

'Good grief!' he said. 'Well there aren't any there now! Who cleared that area?'

'I think it was Norman,' said Steve.

Gordon pursed his lips and scratched his head.

'What are we going to do?' asked Norman, panic-stricken.

'We?' asked Gordon.

'Well you should have told me they were there.'

'I tried, remember? You told me you knew about bracken and wouldn't let me tell you. You heard, didn't you lads?'

'Oh yes,' Donald and Steve said, nodding their heads, trying to keep straight faces.

'Fine friends you are,' Norman said, his brow furrowed, his mouth down at the corners and his eyes wide.

'You've never seen Frank when he's really angry, have you Donald?' said Gordon. 'He's fearsome! I tell you what you could do, Norman. If I can find one, you can plant it again. He'll never know what happened.'

'That's an idea,' said Norman, cheering up.

Gordon reluctantly got to his feet and started rummaging through the pile of bracken. He put one aside, then after more rummaging two more.

'If we plant these three, at least one should take,' he said. 'The roots aren't too badly damaged. If they don't take we can blame the foxes.'

'Oh good, thank you, thank you,' babbled the relieved Norman, taking the bracken and rushing over to the area he had cleared.

'Would here do?' he called out.'

'About a metre to the right,' said Gordon, pouring another cup of tea from his flask. 'Put them all together.'

'Are you going to let him plant them?' asked Steve incredulously.

'Why not,' said Gordon. 'He wouldn't listen to me. It will teach him a lesson. Whoops, here's Frank.'

The warden came towards them, looking at Norman busily planting the bracken.

'What's he doing?'

'Well we keep pulling the bracken up and he keeps planting it again,' said Gordon. 'I really don't know why. We'd better get back to work before he plants it all and we have to pull the whole lot up again.'

'One day someone is going to take exception to your jokes,' said Frank, grinning despite himself. 'I'll put him out of his misery.'

He walked over to the unfortunate Norman, who had planted one and was trying to hide the other two.

'Sorry Frank, I really didn't know there was any *Brackonium willmottiae* here,' he said miserably. 'The others didn't tell me, but I think it will be all right, the roots are not badly damaged.'

'Norman, there's no such thing as *Brackonium willmottiae*. It's just bracken. It's only one of Gordon's jokes.'

'You bastards!' said Norman, shaking his head. Then seeing the funny side, he started laughing. 'You bastards,' he repeated.

'OK, fun's over,' said Frank. 'I'll stay and finish off with Steve, you three go and help at the reservoir.'

'Oh no!' cried Gordon and Norman, while Donald looked on puzzled at their reaction.

'The reservoir is that big concrete pond just by the coach house,' explained Gordon as they made their way through the undergrowth.

'What, that one about four metres deep, with a little bit of water at the bottom?'

'That's right. There's about a foot of water but a good foot of sludge too, along with branches fallen from the trees and rubble from goodness knows where. We have to clear it every so often, but we never finish it. There's far too much in there.'

They reached the area at the same time as the team that had been clearing it before the break.

'Good to see you,' grinned David. 'The waders are over there.'

'God it stinks!' said Donald as the smell from a pile of sludge wafted his way. He looked over the edge of the concrete wall that projected about a metre above ground level. What water there was seemed an awful long way down, three or four metres he guessed. Ivy hung thickly over the wall except at one end where it had been cleared for buckets of sludge to be hauled up. There was also a gap at the other end where a ladder had been placed.

'I'll go down first,' said Gordon to Donald's surprise, picking up one pair of waders. 'Don't want Susan getting uptight if you go back stinking. Come on Norman, put the other pair on.'

Donald wandered off to the other end where a couple of buckets had been tied to lengths of rope. He took one and David the other, then when Gordon and Norman had descended the ladder and splashed their way across he and David lowered the two buckets.

After sloshing sounds and considerable moans from both of them, Gordon and Norman stood back while the buckets were hauled to the top.

'Strewth these are heavy,' gasped Donald as he pulled his over the top of the wall and carried it to the other side of the path before tipping the foul looking contents out.

'Coming down,' he called, looking over the edge before lowering his bucket back down. The water was still bubbling from where it had been disturbed.

Gordon fished about in the water and pulled up a large piece of wood and threw it in to the corner, hundreds more bubbles coming to the surface.

By the end of the hour Donald's arms were aching and his trousers were covered in black slime that had splashed him when emptying his bucket. It must be lunch time soon, he thought. Then, looking over before lowering his bucket once more he saw Gordon making for the ladder while Norman was still filling his bucket. He walked round to ask what was happening and got there in time to see his friend pulling his waders off and putting on his boots.

'I've had enough,' he said. Then he grinned and put his finger to his lips, then reaching over the side quietly pulled the aluminium ladder up from the water and laid it down on the path.

'Lunch time!' he called out, then crouched down by the wall.

David came round, saw what was happening and grinned. 'He really shouldn't be down there on his own,' he said. 'It's very slippery and quite dangerous.'

Just at that moment there was a cry and a splash. They jumped up and looked over to see ripples rushing away from the centre of the reservoir and bubbles shooting up all round.

'Oh shit!' said Gordon, frantically lifting the ladder and dropping it back over the side. Jumping over, he slid down rather than using the rungs. The sludge and water came up to his knees as he splashed as fast as he could to where the bubbles still rose to the surface.

'What are you doing? My goodness, you're getting very wet.'

The voice came from underneath the ivy next to the ladder, where Norman huddled safe in his waders.

'You... you...' spluttered Gordon, unable to think of a suitable comment.

'Oh no! You didn't think that was me did you? I just cleared a branch away from here and threw it over there.'

'I suppose we are even now,' suggested Norman when they had both got to the top and pulled the ladder up.

'No, not even,' said Gordon reluctantly, looking down at his soaking wet trousers. 'I think you won today hands down.'

20

The filmy-fern cave enables Alex to remember his name

'Remember when I first came you said we could look in the filmy-fern cave?' asked Alex, pointing to a door blocking the mouth of a cave in the side of the gorge. 'Can we do it now?'

That the cave, about eight feet high and the same across at its widest, was man-made was obvious from the glazed roof and metal supporting structure, but the walls comprised huge rocks with water-loving plants growing out of every crevice.

'Ah, the filmy-fern cave,' said Jacob. 'A magical place. Very well, come on, I'll show you. Be careful though – for the plants' sake as well as your own. Some of them are irreplaceable.'

He started climbing down the ten feet or so, carefully stepping from one rock to the next, stopping from time to time to look at a plant that might need attention later.

Alex froze. Another piece of the jig-saw was falling into place. He remembered just once going to a meeting in the trenches. They wanted him to do a special reconnaissance trip in his Camel and he was to be briefed by the army. They'd scrambled along a trench to a very deep dug-out in which the senior officers did their planning. Far enough back to be reasonably safe, but only compared with the real front line. Near enough for the earth to shake when the shells came in. Near enough to be hit by one. But hopefully deep enough not to be blown to smithereens by a lucky – or unlucky, depending on your point of view – strike.

He remembered the mud most of all. And it wasn't even the depths of winter. How on earth did those poor devils stand it, day in day out – no, month in, month out? If they were really lucky, year in year out – but very few were that lucky. Hearing the shriek of an incoming shell, hoping it had some other poor sod's name on it, not theirs, and throwing themselves into muddy funk-holes.

Then at a time determined by some nice clean staff-officer in his nice safe dug-out way back, or even from his room in London, they had to climb out of their filthy refuges and walk towards the enemy machine guns hoping that they would get a nice bullet through an arm or a leg as a ticket home. If they could make it back to their lines that is. Of course the nice convenient wound might get infected in which case they could lose their arm or their leg; or their life.

He could see the Lt-Colonel now, welcoming him in that fashion that could have been friendly or could have been patronising, you never could decide. 'Hello Charles,' he was saying, 'come on in.'

'You all right Alex?'

He hesitated for a moment, inclined to tell Jacob that he had remembered what his real name was, but something stopped him. There was no harm in letting Jacob carry on calling him Alex, at least until he had fully recovered his memory. But a deep fear kept bubbling up. He didn't want to remember it all. The fear was that he would, like it or not.

'I'm fine,' he said, following Jacob down. 'It just reminded me of the trenches, that's all.'

'Oh no, I didn't think of that,' apologised Jacob. 'It's really not worth seeing, let's get back up.'

'No, I'd like to see it. I don't want to spend the rest of my life missing out on things because they remind me of the war.'

'If you are sure,' said Jacob, stepping into the shallow water, turning a big key in the lock and heaving open the heavy wooden door to the cave. 'It's a bit gloomy and you'll get your feet wet, but in you come.'

After a suspicious look at the big rocks forming the lintel to the opening Alex ducked through, closing the door behind him.

'This is fantastic,' he whispered.

'No need to whisper,' laughed Jacob. 'But it does have that effect on you, doesn't it?'

It was hot and humid. Uncomfortably hot and humid, but fitting for what it was. The rocks forming the walls and part of the roof were huge, glistening and dripping with water. Brought from Yorkshire at enormous expense, Jacob said. And from every crack and crevice a plant grew. They were mostly ferns, small ones, many with strange translucent leaves, but other plants too. Alex hadn't a clue what they were and didn't ask. Not only would the names not mean a thing to him, it would spoil the 'feel' of the cave. To him it wasn't about how rare the plants were, what

125

species or genus, even what each one looked like. The overall effect was magical.

'It's beautiful.'

'I knew you'd like it,' smiled Jacob, waiting while Alex's eyes roamed over the cavern and its plants.

'We'd better go back up,' he suggested eventually. 'Her Ladyship will be wondering where we are.'

'Yes, I have noticed that she wanders about the garden keeping an eye on us all,' said Alex wryly.

'I don't think it's just that. She loves her garden and never loses an opportunity to go round it and see how her plants are getting on. We are all incidental to that and she can't understand why sometimes we need to stop for a while.'

They carefully retraced their footsteps to the top.

'Unless you've something else for me I might just get back to the walled garden,' said Alex as they stood looking down at the stream rippling gently round the rocks. 'The south wall really is in a bit of a state. We could really do with some new bricks but perhaps she can't afford them.'

'No, it's not that,' explained Jacob. 'She just doesn't like new bricks, especially in among so many old ones. It does make life difficult but the result is worth it, don't you think?'

Alex nodded, but his eyes were suddenly wary as he looked at the sky for the source of the noise. An aeroplane was about to intrude upon their peace. A Sopwith Camel from the sound of it. He knew it so well and didn't want to know it at all. He covered his ears but couldn't help looking. It was quite high, but suddenly dipped its nose and dived towards them, its engine note rising to a crescendo.

The deep dark despair enveloped him as he crouched down and put his arms over his head. He wasn't frightened of the aeroplane, there was something else. Something much worse. He saw the pilot's head disappearing as machine gun bullets hit it. The nightmare he had experienced time and time again, leaving him shaking and in tears.

The aeroplane pulled its nose up and it rose into a loop, before rolling off the top and disappearing over the horizon.

'Why do they keep doing that,' cried Alex. 'Why here?'

'I think it's not us, it's the Warley Barracks,' explained Jacob. 'It's probably some sort of navigation point too. Or maybe they just like to look at the garden!'

But Alex wasn't in the mood for frivolity, not now. That dark secret was getting too near the surface for comfort. He wanted to lock it safely away.

'Some people say the only way to get rid of your fears is to face them,' said Jacob. 'I used to be frightened of spiders, which is a problem if you are a gardener. But my love of gardening was greater than my fears of spiders and I found out more about them. I developed quite an interest in them and now I have no fear at all.'

'I have a feeling that my fear is something else entirely,' said Alex slowly. 'I am afraid of finding out what it is, let along facing up to it.'

'Well if you want to talk about it at any time, just say,' said Jacob. 'I won't push you.'

Alex walked off to the wall, still shaking and deep in thought. Jacob was probably right. Ellen Willmott had said much the same thing, and so had Dr Townsend. They were all knowledgeable people, particularly Dr Townsend, but even so he had an awful feeling that they might be wrong.

Pulling out a couple of loose bricks he started chipping away at the old mortar so that he could bed them in again properly. Ellen Willmott hated new bricks so he had to put the old ones back again – ravaged as they were by time and the weather. Pretty much like him and others like him, he thought. Ravaged by time and the weather if they were lucky; ravaged by bullets or gas if they weren't. If she had to replace the old bricks with new ones Ellen Willmott insisted on them being smeared with cattle dung. This made them look older and encouraged the growth of lichen which further enhanced the effect. Pity it wasn't so easy with human beings.

Much of the mortar was in need of attention and with thoughts of the war receding, he was soon at peace with the world as he chipped and scraped.

'You've made a real difference to this place,' came the now familiar high pitched voice from behind him.

'I'm glad,' he replied, turning to her. 'This place and the people in it have made a real difference to me.'

'In what way?'

'Well I am learning things that I have previously taken for granted. Mostly about plants, but also about what is really important in life. Every day Jacob teaches me a little more and I find that most enjoyable.'

'Yes, Jacob is a good teacher. His enthusiasm is infectious. Has he taught you the most basic thing of all?'

Alex looked puzzled.

'What is a plant?'

Alex smiled.

'Well, no, he hasn't mentioned that yet. I have never asked because I thought it was obvious, but you wouldn't have mentioned it if that were the case.'

'That's right. Try to work it out then,' she suggested.

'Well the obvious things are that a plant is static, it needs sunlight, water and nutrients. It has leaves, flowers and roots. And it makes seeds. I can't think of anything else.'

'Not bad. But some plants don't make flowers. Conifers, for instance, and ferns. Some cacti don't appear to have leaves. Are fungi plants? They produce spores that are like seeds but don't get their energy from sunlight, nor do other parasitic plants.'

'So what is the definition?' asked Alex.

'I'm not sure that there is an exact definition. Even Doctor Johnson had trouble being specific in his excellent dictionary. Some people say a plant is a static organism that takes its food in water solution, but what about carnivorous plants? I mention it only to give your fertile brain something on which to ponder.'

'Thank you. Another lesson, too – not to take things for granted.' His brow furrowed. 'I remembered my name earlier today, when at the fern cave with Jacob. My Christian name, anyway. I didn't tell Jacob. Was that wrong?'

'No, not wrong and don't tell me what it is either. I may be asked and I don't want to have to lie, so keep it from Jacob for the same reason. Unless you feel the need to tell either of us, that is.'

'No, I'm quite happy to be known as Alex. But it has raised a question in my mind. As I have said on a number of occasions, I am very happy here. Do I want to remember my past and to go back to a life that may not allow me so much contentment? Why not draw a line under it and go on from here?'

'I would be delighted to have you here, you know I would, and so would everyone else. But you could never guarantee that your past would not come back to haunt you. Anyway, what about the beautiful woman in the photograph that you carry with you, would you not miss her? Is she not missing you?'

'Yes,' he admitted. 'I think if it wasn't for her I would be sorely tempted to do as I have said and simply start life afresh. Many of the soldiers in the war will never have that opportunity.'

'Anyway,' she said hopefully, 'just because you take up your old life it does not mean you have to break with this one. I would always welcome you back, if you chose to visit.'

'Of course! Why did I jump to the conclusion that it might be otherwise?'

'My dear mother used to say,' said Ellen Willmott. 'Eat your greens first. Then you will enjoy the roast potatoes even more afterwards. It is the same with life. Face up to the unpleasant things first, solve the difficult problems before doing anything else, then you will be able to really enjoy the pleasures that follow.'

'That's so true,' he said thoughtfully.

'Well, don't work too late. And don't forget. Any time you wish to talk, I would be glad to listen.'

'Thank you again, Miss Willmott.'

She looked quickly around. They were alone.

'It's Ellen,' she said. 'When the men are not here, it's Ellen.'

21

Alex at last faces his Demons

'No point in making a mix now Alex, you might as well finish.'

Alex jumped. He hadn't heard Jacob coming, so engrossed was he.

'I'm all right,' he said. 'I'll hang on for half an hour to clean out this last bit, then tomorrow I can start pointing straight away.'

'You really do enjoy that, don't you.'

Alex pondered for a moment.

'Yes. I like everything I do here.'

'OK. Mind the plants though, she'll have a real tantrum if you tread on any.'

'I'll be careful,' promised Alex as he got back to his work.

'Everything all right here?'

'Yes thank-you Miss Willmott,' said Jacob. 'I was just trying to get Alex to finish but he's staying for a bit.'

'You've done more than your bit Alex,' she said. 'Why not take Jacob's advice and call it a day?'

'Because I enjoy it here,' he said. 'I've started writing a journal and sometimes I write it here rather than back at the bothy. I hope that's all right?'

'By all means. But don't give any of my secrets away! I'll get Robinson to send some sandwiches out.'

Jacob's eyes opened slightly wider at hearing this comment and he made his way back to South Lodge while Ellen Willmott took the short walk to the house.

Alex smiled and picked up his hammer and chisel, his thoughts far away as the pieces of mortar flew out under his steady blows. Several bricks were loose so he took them out, cleaned them up and did the same for the cavity they left.

It took a little longer than he had envisaged, as these things often do, but by the end of the hour he had finished. That section of wall was ready for mortaring, but it could wait until the morning. He put his tools down and was surprised to see the sandwiches and a glass of water near him, placed quietly down by the ever considerate Robinson.

As he munched his sandwiches and ran through in his mind what he would write in his journal he wondered what it was that he liked so much about this place and the people who worked here. There were so few now. He knew that up to a hundred people were employed there at one time and they were all kept fully occupied. Those left couldn't help but know that it was a lost cause but must have loved it all as much as he did. Why on earth was that?

Ellen Willmott herself was of course a charismatic person. She could be sharp at times and was totally naïve about money, but so talented. The staff all not only feared and respected her, they also loved her. He had heard that she had time for them not only when she was admonishing them; she would also stop and talk if she met them outside the estate – which usually meant on her walk back from the station after one of her London trips.

Alex didn't know Robinson very well, but he was obviously devoted to her and knew what she wanted often before she did herself.

As for Jacob, well everyone loved Jacob. He was a quiet person, but always ready to help and his enjoyment in teaching others about alpine gardens in general and this one in particular was plain for all to see. The prospect of developing a garden such as this would have been enough on its own to entice him from his native Switzerland, but the promise of taking over the south lodge with a little pension when he retired had clinched it. Alex wondered, though, whether either would be possible given a financial position that necessitated laying off so many staff and making savings that resulted in the deterioration of much of the garden.

Restless, but unwilling to go back to the cold bothy, he got to his feet and made his way out of the walled garden to look at the greenhouses and cold frames. Several panes of glass were broken and the woodwork needed a good coat of paint but he knew it would never happen.

A movement attracted his attention and he looked down at one of the many dip tanks that were scattered throughout the garden. Buried galvanised tanks with open tops, they were filled either from rainfall or from a tanker wheeled round from time to time and used for ad hoc watering of plants. The water level in this one was several inches below the top and a mouse was swimming in it, unable to get out. Alex reached in, took hold of the mouse's tail and lifted it clear, setting it carefully down in the grass. He smiled as he watched it scamper away to safety. It was strange how good that made him feel. He knew that the mouse wasn't grateful to him, it probably didn't know what had happened and certainly not why. It was good sometimes just to help other beings without thought of reward.

He walked on, feeling happier now.

The turkey oak and the Caucasian wing-nut tree both looked regal. Solid; dependable. A pity the daffodils weren't out on the daffodil bank, nor the bluebells. This part of the garden really was looking neglected – even the boating lake, which must have been a real sight when the garden was in its prime, was looking dowdy with weeds spreading out over the water and the banks overgrown.

Climbing up the slope by the north pond, he turned and made his way to the sweet chestnut trees and then on to the alpine garden that he loved almost as much as Jacob did.

With light beginning to fade he turned and made his way back to the walled garden, ready now to complete his journal entry for the day.

He sat down on his tool box, pulled out his notebook and pencil and started to write.

The strains of Ellen Willmott's Amati violin came floating across the garden and he shut his eyes to let the beautiful music soak into his soul. Why did music have that effect on people, he wondered. Well on him, anyway.

The piece ended and he sat there listening to the sounds about him. A rabbit came close, saw him and ran back to its burrow. Ellen Willmott had given up trying to get rid of them and Alex had never tried. They were creatures put on this earth, they can enjoy it alongside us, he thought.

Then the familiar notes of the piano broke the night. He was suddenly frightened. He had no idea why, but he had an awful premonition.

'Tis the last rose of summer, left blooming all alone.
All her lovely companions, are faded and gone.

He saw as clearly as if she were there a vision of a beautiful slim young woman with long black hair singing while he himself played the piano.

'Olivia,' he whispered to himself. 'Olivia. What has happened to me? Why am I here?'

The memories started seeping back: The musical evening, the walk down to the lake, together with her in the summer house. Wasn't someone else with them?

His own name was Charles, he knew that now, but who was this other person?

He remembered going back to that awful war. His Sopwith Camel, a frightening dog fight with all those Germans. Hit in the leg by a machine gun bullet. He rolled his trouser leg up – yes, there was the scar.

He'd been scared before, but not like this.

Harry, that was his name, it was Harry who started out with them down to the lake; Olivia's brother. Why had he blanked that out? Dear Harry, who had tactfully gone off to watch his badgers so that they could be on their own before he went back to the war.

There was a special mission. It was supposed to have been an easy one, but he'd been shot down, he remembered that now.

He remembered seeing that pilot's head disintegrating under his machine gun fire. He cringed at the thought. Why did mankind think up so many awful ways to kill each other? Evil, so evil. But we had to stand up to the Kaiser. There was no alternative. All those people getting killed. In the trenches, on the sea, in the air.

Why did he have to kill too?

Face up to the unpleasant things, that was what Ellen Willmott had said. Then you can enjoy the pleasures that follow.

He thought again about that poor pilot, the blood, flesh and bone disappearing in the slipstream.

The memory hit him like a hammer blow. He started to cry.

Eventually he picked up his pencil and started to write, stopping only from time to time to wipe the tears from his eyes.

22

A Dreadful Day for all concerned

Jacob stepped out of South Lodge into the early morning sun. Six o'clock was when the gardeners had always started work when James Preece was the Head Gardener and when Ellen Willmott was at Warley she was usually out and about at that time to make sure standards had not slipped. He didn't mind anyway, the morning was his best time, but some of the young lads did. Not that there were many of them left now.

He trudged up the stony driveway. The hornbeam was doing well. Goodness knows how old it was, two hundred years, maybe three. The oak too, that was well over a hundred years old. They had started life so long before him and would still be there long after he was gone. But the flowers, ah, that was different. Already parts of the estate were reverting to wilderness. There just weren't enough gardeners to keep it up. How long would it be before the sycamores, the nettles and the brambles took over? Poor Ellen Willmott, it must be breaking her heart to see it going like this.

Instead of turning left to his workplace he carried on, pausing at the turning circle in front of the house to gaze across at the walnut tree. Alex had finished the shuttering, it only needed filling with cement and the tree should be safe for a few years yet.

He turned by the *Umbellularia californica*. The headache tree. Ellen Willmott used to crush the leaves in her fingers and let visitors take in the pungent smell before telling them it gave people a headache. Whether it was psychological or a real effect, they often did soon complain of a headache. The estate was becoming one big headache now though, thought Jacob.

Shaking himself out of his morbid mood he continued the circular route towards his beloved alpine garden. Past the walled garden – Alex had done well repairing that too, he had been a real asset over these last weeks – and by the chestnuts. He barely glanced at the view over London. A dirty smoky place, in his opinion, not worth a first look let alone a second.

At last his flowers came into sight, nestling among the rocks right down to the stream itself. This truly was his Garden of Eden.

Were they weeds growing down there by the water? He carefully picked his way down and pulled the offending intruders out of the crevice into which they had settled themselves.

He looked back towards the bridge over the gorge and felt his knees start to buckle.

'No!' he shouted. 'No! No!'

A body was hanging from a rope tied to the handrail. Alex's body.

Tears already pouring down his cheeks and oblivious now of his precious plants he scrambled up the side of the gorge to the bridge, taking out his knife as he did so.

'Jacob, are you all right?' he heard in the distance.

'Here Miss Willmott, quickly,' he shouted. 'By the bridge.'

He knew that they could never pull Alex up from there so as his mistress came panting up he left his knife there and rushed back down below the bridge to break Alex's fall.

Summing up the situation immediately Ellen Willmott took the knife and sawed through the rope. Jacob had just managed to reach the legs and collapsed in the stream with Alex's lifeless body on top of him. Fortunately unhurt he dragged it clear of the water as Ellen Willmott joined him. They immediately saw that any attempt to revive him would be useless. He must have done this terrible thing the previous evening.

'Whatever are we to do Miss Ellen?' whispered Jacob. 'Why should he have done such a thing?'

'He was certainly a very disturbed man. War does terrible things to a person's mind. Look in his pockets Jacob, he may have left a note.'

Jacob hesitated. It didn't seem right, going through someone else's pockets. But Miss Willmott was right, he may have left something.

'He was always writing in a notebook,' he said. 'I suppose there might be something in there.'

She nodded impatiently.

Then he saw it – a package bobbing precariously by a rock, about to be swept away. It must have fallen from his pocket when they cut him down. Jacob made a grab for it but slipped and it floated quickly out into the current on its way to the South Pond.

'Quickly man!'

135

He hurriedly jumped back into the stream and waded after it, but the current was too fast. Each time it seemed to hold fast by a rock or a fern it swept away just before he reached it. Then when all seemed to be lost it caught an eddy and swung into the filmy fern cave.

Gasping for breath and freezing cold Jacob gratefully picked it up and returned to Miss Willmott.

It was, as they had suspected, Alex's notebook.

Ellen Willmott took it from Jacob and opened it. There was a soggy but perfectly readable note inside, which she read out loud.

"*Dear Jacob,*" it started.

She made no attempt to pass it to Jacob.

"*I am so very sorry to have done this to you. You have all been so kind to me. You, Miss Willmott, Robinson, everyone. I owe you an explanation at least.*

"*I expect you will from time to time have wondered whether I really had lost my memory, or whether it was just a pretence to avoid my responsibilities.*"

'No, never,' protested Jacob.

'Sh!'

"*I could indeed remember very little of my life over the past year. Things came back to me bit by bit, but there was always something there that frightened me. Something I did not want to face. But you were right, I did need to face my demons. One can not live one's life avoiding unpleasant truths.*

"*You may remember that I was involved in a particularly difficult air battle against German fighters. You may remember that I was horrified at the sight of my bullets blowing apart another pilot's head.*

"*Oh dear, the memory, that dreadful memory, I can hardly bear to think about it.*"

'The poor man,' choked Jacob.

'Quiet!'

"*I have to say it. I have to. That pilot was not a German, though that would have been bad enough. That pilot was my friend, my fiancée's brother, Harry. Oh my God, what have I done?*"

Jacob cried out. Ellen Willmott looked away, but not before he had seen her own wet cheeks. After a pause she carried on.

"I did not mean to do it, you will know that I am sure. But in aerial combat things happen so fast. I was frightened, surrounded by enemy aeroplanes, all shooting at me. I shot at anything, not expecting my friend to be there in front of me..

"I don't want to die but I am more frightened of living. Fortunately those close to me must have thought I had perished in the crash that followed.

"So I can only thank you all but leave you now.

"I bequeath to you my journal, Jacob. You will see that my real name still does not appear in its pages. This is because you and Miss Willmott are good and truthful people. If those in authority came and asked what had happened then you may have felt honour bound to tell them, so in an effort to keep you from that unenviable position I would prefer to continue with the name by which you know me.

"It may be that in the far future someone will be able to understand, and something within me wants to leave some sort of clue so that the truth may not be lost forever. I have therefore hidden the photograph you have already seen. On its back I have written the names of the two of us – my dearest beloved fiancée and myself. Should you solve this clue too soon I beg you not to contact them. It is better that they continue to believe that I died in that crash rather than like this.

"One last favour I ask. There will be malicious tongues who may cast doubts upon this remarkable establishment that has given me so much in these last weeks. Should you feel able to do so, could you not bury me quietly somewhere in view of the alpine garden? The authorities need only believe that I departed in the night, where to you do not know. This may not be too far from the truth.

"The clue then, for someone in the far future, is this:

"The truth can be found from mixing her humnobium seeds."

"I am sure that a just God would allow me to meet you all again some day, as I also hope to meet my sweet fiancée. Meanwhile, my good friend, farewell."

Ellen Willmott was by now making no attempt to hide her grief and in a rare moment of emotion they hugged each other until the sobbing subsided.

'We must do it, Jacob. Do as he asked. You and I, we will bury him here as he requested. Hide his body with ferns and start digging deep. I will go to direct the staff to other areas of the garden.'

Wiping her eyes, she gave Jacob the letter and journal and hustled off.

'You, Maurice, what are you doing here?' he heard her say. 'Over to the cold frames, they are in a dreadful state. And you Max, the North Pond needs weeding.'

He gently covered his friend's body with ferns, tears dropping on to the waxen face.

'It was an accident Alex. No-one would blame you except you yourself. War is like that. Innocent people get killed all the time. She would have understood, she knew he was your friend.'

He picked up his spade.

'Where would you like to go, dear friend?'

He looked about.

'It matters little. Your spirit will wander this place when you want peace. We will follow you soon enough, then perhaps we can talk some more and I can continue to teach you the names of these wonderful flowers.'

He carefully lifted some plants, and set them aside. Then he started to dig. With slow sweeps of his spade the pile of earth mounted on the path and the hole grew deeper. Eventually it was to his satisfaction and he stood back, resting for a moment.

'Have you done then, Jacob?' She had returned.

'Yes Miss Willmott.'

'Excuse us Alex,' said Jacob as they dragged his body to the hole in the ground. 'Neither of us is as strong as we used to be.'

They gave it a final push and it twisted and fell in an untidy heap. Jacob eased himself in beside the body and straightened it out. Illogically he brushed dirt from the cold forehead and looked up at Ellen Willmott.

'I'm sorry Miss Willmott, I can't just throw earth over him like this. Can we cover him?'

Her normally severe face softened and she undid her apron, passing it down to Jacob who covered Alex's face and body with it. He then undid his own apron and covered the rest before climbing out of the hole.

'Goodbye Alex, old friend,' he whispered and started heaving the earth back in until the body was covered.

'Can I put a rock over it?'

138

'Do whatever you wish. But don't say a word to anyone about what we have done. Already I am wondering if we have done the right thing. Don't make it look like a grave either, or someone will dig it up to find out.'

'I'll say you wanted a setting for some flowers.'

'What flowers?'

'*Primula sikkimensis* I think. They were the first flowers he learned to identify here.'

'If you wish,' she grunted, turning away. 'Remember, not a word.'

He watched as she stalked off. He also saw the handkerchief taken surreptitiously from her pocket to dab at her eyes and quickly replaced. Then she took out her little notebook and jotted something down before disappearing back into the house.

'Oh Alex,' he whispered. 'You were here for such a short time and you made such an impression on us all. Why, oh why, didn't you see it through?'

He looked thoughtfully at the journal. Poor Alex, what did he mean by *her humnobium seeds*? Whose? Ellen Willmott's presumably. Jacob had never heard of such a plant, but although his knowledge was extensive no-one could know them all. Perhaps it was a new one that she had brought back from one of her travels and didn't want anyone to know. Anyway, he really wasn't sure that he wanted to know who the real Alex was. The one he knew at Warley Place was real enough.

Miss Willmott no doubt thought the journal had been buried with Alex. He couldn't keep it though, there was nowhere to hide it at South Lodge. Where could he put it? He couldn't just bury it, it would rot or animals would dig it up. Then he had an idea.

He opened it at the last page, added a few lines and trudged to his shed. Wrapping the journal and its letter in several layers of oiled cloth, he entered the walled garden and walked its full length to the part which Alex had almost completely restored. Levering a couple of loose bricks out, then making a hole in the rubble-filled cavity, he pushed the journal in and replaced the bricks. Making up a small amount of lime mortar mix, he carefully fixed them in place.

Perhaps someone, someone who will understand, someone in the distant future, will find this, he thought. Someone who will understand what Alex was really like. What a good man he was.

Someone who could see past the suicide and see the tortured mind beneath. A mind tortured because it cared too much.

He did not see the curtain at an upstairs window drop back into place as he washed his trowel and with a heavy heart turned to make his way back to the alpine garden. No, not yet, he thought and instead turned left to leave the garden by the nursery beds and the greenhouses. A movement caught his eye and he looked down to see a vole climbing out of a dip tank using a piece of wood wedged in so that it did not float. He walked on to see another branch in the next tank, and another.

For some reason this act of kindness, which he knew must have been one of Alex's last acts in the garden, made him immeasurably sad. How awful when a man so dedicated to the wellbeing not only of his fellow human beings but also to the lower animals could be driven to end his life in such a way. He turned and started to make his way back to his alpine garden but stopped as he heard the familiar sound of Ellen Willmott's violin. She was also singing.

'Tis the last rose of summer, Left blooming all alone,
All her lovely companions Are faded and gone.
No flower of her kindred, No rose bud is nigh,
To reflect back her blushes, Or give sigh for sigh.

How sad, thought Jacob as he turned to continue his journey.

I'll not leave thee, thou lone one, To pine on the stem;

He stopped in mid stride. How extraordinary. She never sang the second verse.

Since the lovely are sleeping, Go sleep thou with them;
Thus kindly I scatter Thy leaves o'er the bed
Where thy mates of the garden Lie scentless and dead.

Alex's death must have hit her really hard. The pity was that she seemed so afraid of showing her emotions.

So soon may I follow When friendships decay,
And from love's shining circle The gems drop away!

When true hearts lie withered And fond ones are flown
Oh! who would inhabit This bleak world alone?

There was a deathly silence as the notes faded away. Even the birds seemed to have stopped singing, as if unable to compete with the beauty of the music.

Jacob shook his head sadly at the thought of Ellen Willmott alone in her room with her Amati violins, her books, her furniture, her pictures, nothing but the best of everything. But the one thing she wanted above all else, someone to care for, had been suddenly and cruelly taken away and no money on earth could bring it back. He doubted that she would ever get over this day and knew for certain that they would never hear her sing that song again.

23

The Clue

'Well that's that finished,' said Donald, saving the file on his computer and carefully closing the journal. 'I feel so sorry for him. It must have been bad enough for anyone caught up in that war, but to accidentally kill your best friend, that's awful.'

'Killed his best friend? How?'

'Yes, that was his dark secret. It was in a dog fight. His aircraft and his friend's had been attacked by a number of Germans. It was a real mess and when he fired his guns he accidentally shot his friend and saw his head fly into pieces.'

'Oh God! How awful, the poor man! I can understand why he killed himself,' said Susan looking up from her crossword. 'Did he ever say what his name was?'

'No, he was too afraid that someone would find out and think the worst of him. He preferred them to think he had been killed in that air fight.'

'So we'll never know?'

'Not unless we can solve the clue that he left. Fat chance of that now, after all these years. And I don't know the first thing about botany so I think I'll just let it rest.'

'Clue? What clue? Can I see it?'

'Of course dear. You know more about botany than I do. What do you think?'

He passed the copy of Alex's note to Susan and carefully put the original copy of the journal in a padded envelope to take to the next Monday's meeting.

"The truth can be found from mixing her humnobium seeds." she read. 'It's like a crossword clue.'

'Did they have crosswords in those days?'

'No, but they were very fond of word games. This looks like an anagram.'

'How on earth can you tell that?'

'It says 'mixing her humnobium seeds'. The word 'mixing' often denotes an anagram. I'll play with it for a bit.'

'You could be right,' said Donald thoughtfully. 'I looked 'humnobium' up in the dictionary and searched for it on the computer but couldn't find anything. Worth a try, anyway. Meanwhile I'll get on with stripping the wallpaper in the spare room.'

'No, don't worry, it'll last another year at least. How about taking me round Warley Place again? It's a lovely evening, too good for working.'

'I'd love to if you're sure.'

'I'm sure.'

He grabbed the car keys and went to the door.

'Donald,' she said.

'Yes?'

'In your slippers?'

'Oh God!' He hurried up the stairs to the bedroom and came down with a pair of trainers in his hand.

They didn't say a word all the way to Warley Place – he deep in thought, wondering at how much things had improved between them and why, she busy looking at the jumble of letters scribbled on a piece of paper.

The moorhens came hurrying out looking for their breadcrumbs and the cows looked up mournfully as they got out of the car and made for the swing gate.

'I'm really looking forward to the spring,' Susan said softly, looking at the East Meadow on their right as they strolled up the path. 'The crocuses on that field are supposed to be a fantastic sight. Or used to be. I don't remember seeing them for the past few years.'

'Have you been here in spring before?' Donald asked, puzzled. 'I thought when you came with me that was the first time.'

'No, I've just seen them through gaps in the trees as we've driven past. I hadn't realised we were allowed to go in. It was the first time when I was with you.'

They wandered on up the driveway in silence until they came to the turning circle and stood looking at the old cellar, trying to imagine what the house would have looked like had it still been standing.

Donald glanced to his left.

'That's a Headache Tree.'

'A what?!'

'It's an Oregon Myrtle, but it's called a headache tree because if you crush the leaves and smell them it gives you a headache. So they say.'

'I don't think I'll try it,' she laughed, putting her arm round him. 'Oh look, a *Verbascum*.'

'A what?'

'Mullein.'

'Sorry, you've lost me.'

'Yellow Verbascum is common, but that one looks a sort of pinky white.'

She pushed her way through the bushes to get a closer look.

'It's a bit late for them so most of them are dead now, but there's just a few flowers on this one.'

She pushed her way out back to Donald, her face animated. He wondered why she hadn't spotted them on their previous visit.

On they walked, her eyes flicking to and fro, naming many of the flowers for him and expressing puzzlement at others.

'I had no idea you knew so much about flowers,' he said eventually. 'Why don't you join the gardening group? They go round once a month keeping an eye on the plants and identifying the rare ones. You'd love it.'

'No, Warley Place is your refuge,' she said. 'You can get away from me for a bit each week.'

'But I don't want to get away from you. I do the brickwork with Ben, pull up nettles and chop sycamores down with Frank, that sort of thing. I dare not do anything with plants unless I have specific instructions. I'd go and pull up a rare specimen. Anyway, the specialist group only meet once a month.'

'I'll think about it,' she said softly.

They made their way round to the walled garden and gazed at the magnolias, the chusan palm, the ginkgo, the box hedges. Then suddenly they were at the western end of the south wall.

'I remember now, this is where you showed me you found the journal, isn't it.'

'Yes, just there.'

He pointed to some bricks now indistinguishable from those surrounding them.

'How do you know? They all look the same to me.'

144

'I made a little mark on the four I took out. I also remember the number for the top right hand brick – eighty-five.'

'Eight across, five down?'

'Right.' He was impressed.

'Why not eight down, five across?'

'Oh. Right. Er....'

'How will you remember the number anyway?'

'It's Ellen Willmott's birthday year. Eighteen fifty-eight.'

They stood there for a few minutes, thinking about the events all that time ago.

'We could go round the whole garden,' he said. There's lots of interest there – some really special trees, remains of greenhouses and cold frames, that sort of thing. It might be dark before we got round though. Shall we take the short route back?'

'I think we'd better.'

They both took a last look at the now freshly mortared bricks before wandering on again, out of the garden and down towards the Spanish chestnuts looking out over London.

The light was definitely beginning to fade and Donald noticed an apprehensive look appearing on his wife's face.

'I forgot to tell you,' he said. 'Remember that moaning sound we heard last time?'

'Could I ever forget it?'

'Well in the old days Ellen Willmott used to set traps for intruders trying to steal her plants. One of our volunteers, David, fixed up an electronic equivalent. He's a bit of a whiz with electronics and climbs trees. He made something that has batteries charged up with solar cells high in the trees and detects people using infra-red detectors. It only works at night and produces a number of random sounds, like cracking twigs as if someone else was there. If that doesn't work there is a sort of moan, and a vague sound of a ghostly voice too.'

'It certainly worked as far as I was concerned!'

'It scared me too,' admitted Donald. 'It's getting a bit dim now, so we can expect some more soon.'

He looked over at London, trying to make out the Dome, the Gherkin, or the buildings at Canary Wharf, but it was too dark and rather misty.

'What's that?' asked Susan.

He turned to her. She was looking away from London, towards the shell of a small brick building.

'That's Ellen Willmott's summer house,' he said. 'Why?'

'A creepy feeling ran up my spine.'

They walked on to the bridge over the gorge.

'Better not get too close to the edge,' said Donald. 'It's getting dark and we don't want any accidents.'

'What's that rock?' She pointed to a large rock at the edge of the garden.

'It's just a rock. Why?'

'It doesn't fit in with the rest. There is a sort of random pattern, if that makes sense. But this one…'

She walked the few yards to it and turned for him to join her.

He put his arm round her waist and felt her do the same.

He suddenly felt sorrow at the way they had been with each other since he retired. Time was precious. All he needed to have done was to think of her a bit more, not get wrapped up in his own wants, realise that she might want her own independence and to do her own thing.

'We've both been very silly,' she said, moving round in front of him and pulling him close.

He put both arms round her and bent his head. They kissed. A long passionate, emotional kiss of an intensity they had not experienced for many a long year.

David's alarm system let out a low 'Ahhhh…'

Their lips parted and they both smiled.

'He sounds quite a friendly ghost,' she laughed as arm-in-arm they walked over the bridge and through the gloom to their car.

'Gin and tonic before bed?' Donald asked.

'Yes please.'

'Should you be drinking while you're taking those pills?' she asked as he set two glasses down.

'I kept forgetting to take them,' he said. 'and felt better rather than worse, so I've stopped taking them altogether now. I don't need them any more.'

'The doctor would be the best judge of that.'

'He'd just play safe and tell me to continue with them for a bit. No, I'll just stop and see what happens.'

'If you're sure.'

She went back to poring over the jumble of letters scribbled on a piece of paper in front of her.

She jotted a word down and crossed some of the letters out.

'I've done it,' she cried. 'I knew there was something eerie about that summer house.'

'What do you mean?' he asked, his brow creased in puzzlement as he put down his drink.

'It's an anagram. *Her humnobium seeds.* It means 'Behind summer house'. He must have hidden something there saying who he really was.'

'You're brilliant,' he said, sitting next to her and kissing her. 'We'll go and look. Tomorrow. You and me.'

'Once the summer house came to mind it was easy,' she explained. 'Take those letters out and the word 'behind' was obvious.'

'Obvious to you, maybe. Not to me.'

She sipped her drink.

'Do you think we should? Look for it, I mean. Do you think he really wanted it to be found?'

'Why would he have hidden it if not? He could have destroyed it. His fiancée must be dead long since, certainly also parents of both sides. And there wouldn't have been any children.'

'Let's sleep on it.'

They rose to their feet to go upstairs.

'You've forgotten your book.'

'I know.'

I think I'll just have another look at the journal,' he said innocently.

'You dare!'

24

Ellen Willmott ponders on the Futility of Life

'It is really lovely to see you Rose. I miss you so much.'

'I miss you too.'

Ellen Willmott's sister, Rose, had married and was now part of the wealthy Berkeley family living in the beautiful Spetchley Park estate.

'I must ask. How is the treatment? Is it painful?'

'Not really painful, but I feel so tired. Radium gives hope where there would have been none before but it has a terrible effect on one.'

'Poor Rose.'

'But what of you, Ellie? You too are looking tired. Looking after this estate on your own, and with the financial worries too, that must be very wearying.'

'My tiredness is of my own making. I have Robinson to look after the house and Jacob to look after the garden. I could quite well leave him to look after the alpine garden with his staff and with a few trusted men I could cope with the remainder if I went to London less. But there are so many things I want to do, Rose.'

'That is a lesson that you have yet to learn, Ellie. One doesn't have to do everything, just because it is there to be done. Your music alone would be enough for most women; the same for your photography. Your garden itself would be too much for anyone else that I know. Add the printing, the astronomy – it is no wonder you struggle at times.'

They sipped at their tea and looked through the conservatory window at the garden.

'Talking of financial worries – '

'No Rose, I won't take a penny.'

'Well what are you to do then?'

'I have resolved to sell Tresserve and Boccanegra now this wretched war is over.'

'Good. Travelling to them must be so tiring.'

'It is not that,' said Ellen Willmott quickly. 'It is just that I do not have the time to visit and it seems such a waste.'

Rose smiled.

'Oh all right, I admit it, I do find visiting tiring and yes the money will be very useful here.'

'Will it be enough?'

Ellen Willmott was silent for a moment.

'If necessary I may let out this estate, but it would have to be to someone who would keep the gardens in their present condition.'

'That person might be hard to find. Things will be difficult as we recover from the war.'

'Maybe, but enough of this sort of talk. Are you fit enough for a walk round the garden?'

'Well just the walled garden. And I'd like a quick look at what Jacob is up to. Perhaps you can introduce me to this new chap, the one who lost his memory?'

'Sadly he has gone.'

'Oh no. Where to? Did he get his memory back?'

Ellen Willmott was silent. This was the moment she dreaded. Should she confide in her sister? If she did not, it would be the first time ever. But with the treatment she was having for her cancer, might she unwittingly blurt out the truth? Poor Rose would never forgive herself if that happened. Anyway, she would be asking Rose to keep a secret from her husband and that wasn't fair on her.

'I don't really know where he went.'

True, she thought. Probably to Heaven, if there was a heaven. Never to Hell, despite what these religious lunatics said about suicides.

'The cad!'

'He was no cad. He was someone who had served his country well and who got precious little reward for it. He was a real gentleman. A gentleman in the true sense of the word. I wish I had got to know him better. I wish...'

'Ellie, you were in love with him!'

'No Rose, not in the way you think. He was a young man, a fine young man. I am a crotchety old woman.'

She silenced Rose's protestation with a wave of her hand, annoyed at the tightness in her throat and the mistiness in her eyes.

149

'No Rose. He was the man I would like to have had forty years ago. Or the son I would like to have had now.'

She sheltered her eyes with her hand, but Rose put her arm round her shaking shoulders.

Suddenly Ellen Willmott rose to her feet, dabbing her eyes with her handkerchief.

'Come, we will miss the best of the weather. I fear rain is due.'

They walked slowly the few yards to the walled garden and sat on one of the benches there taking in the myriad scents that pervaded the air, allowing themselves to be dazzled by the colours, marvelling at the shapes and sizes of the smallest flowers to the largest trees.

Eventually they rose and walked round and across the garden, through the box hedges, under the arches of roses, stopping to smell this flower or admire that one.

She glanced at the wall where Jacob had been at work just two days ago. She was glad he had kept the journal safe. Perhaps one day she would retrieve it.

Completing the circuit she looked enquiringly at her sister.

'A little more. To the chestnuts perhaps. Maybe we can see something of London today.'

They walked along the outside of the wall and turned left to the massive trees standing guard over the view down to the capital city itself. Not that Ellen Willmott looked at it very often. She enjoyed her visits there well enough, but once back here she turned her back on it.

'Do you mind if I sit in the summer house for a while?' asked Rose.

'Of course not.'

Ellen Willmott sat with her sister for a few minutes, then reached into her bag and pulled out her notebook.

'What's that?'

'It's an anagram, I think. I came across it the other day.'

Her brow creased as she looked at the words.

' *mixing her humnobium seeds* ' it said.

She rummaged in her bag for a pencil, then crossed out some of the letters. A slow smile of satisfaction appeared, even though her eyes were still sad. She put the notebook away.

'I'm not really in the mood,' she said. 'I'll just go and look at the outside wall for a moment. It needed repair and I want to know if it has been done.'

'You really can't rest,' laughed Rose. 'Go on then.'

Ellen Willmott pushed her way past the saplings sprouting up round the rear of the small brick building. She looked at the wall. Yes, it had been finished. But didn't the mortar round those bricks look just a little fresher than the rest? She pulled her hatpin out and poked at it, then at the adjacent mortar. Yes, she thought triumphantly, she was right. Lime mortar took a while to set hard and to take its final colour. This was where the answer was, if she wanted to find it. Rose asking to sit in the summer house had triggered the answer to the clue.

She eased her way back round the corner.

'All to your satisfaction?' asked her sister.

'Not quite, but it will do for the moment.'

They sat for a few more minutes until Rose got to her feet.

'You are restless Ellie. I have taken up too much of your time...'

'Never,' cried Ellen Willmott.

'...and I am a little tired. I think I shall lie down for a bit.'

'Are you sure? You know I love to be with you. The garden can wait.'

'No, I mean it. I really am tired. I tire so easily now. I will come out again when I am ready.'

Arm in arm, they walked slowly towards the bridge over the gorge. Rose stopped suddenly.

'That rock. It wasn't there before, was it?'

'No. It didn't really fit where it was so I had it moved.'

'And you put *Primula sikkimensis* round it?'

'Yes. Why not?'

'It looks a little out of place.'

'That is just because it is different. Once you get used to it you will realise how well it is now situated.'

Rose nodded, and they walked on.

'You are cold, Ellie?'

'Sometimes there is a cool updraught from the stream here.'

Rose made no comment.

'It might be quicker and easier to retrace our steps to the house, rather than continue on this longer route,' suggested Ellen Willmott.

'That would be preferable,' confessed Rose.

They walked slowly, stopping now and then to admire the *Campanula lactiflora* with its milky white flowers shaded with light blue, and the *Verbascum nigrum* with its yellow flowers and beautiful purple centres that demanded an inspection through an eye glass. But Ellen Willmott could see her sister was exhausted by the time they reached the house.

Robinson came out to meet them.

'Take Rose to her room, would you Robinson?'

Robinson took her arm and helped her through the door.

Poor Rose. Life was so unfair. Perhaps Buddhists had a point when they spoke of the impermanence of everything. Rose, Warley Place, she herself, everything would change or be gone one day. But was that any reason to give up on life? No, she thought. Even if the flesh and blood Rose departed from this earth the memory would live on. The same for Warley Place; whatever Buddhists preached she would continue to struggle and even if it eventually reverted to jungle, the memory of it in its prime too would survive.

She sat for a minute or two, fidgeting. Then she gave up the battle, put a pencil and paper in her pocket and walked quickly to the shed. Grabbing a chipping hammer and a chisel she strode to the summer house. Pushing her way to the back, she started to chip at the still slightly soft mortar.

She smiled to herself as the bricks came away to reveal a thin package. The narrow rubble-filled cavity had been scraped away to make room for what she knew would be the photograph missing from his belongings.

Carefully removing it, she went into the summer house itself and peeled back the oilskin. As she had thought, it was the photograph of him with his fiancée. She turned it over. On the back was written:-

My name is Charles Everington. My beloved fiancée is Olivia Henderson, daughter of Sir James and Lady Mary Henderson. To my eternal shame and sorrow it was her brother, Harry Henderson, whom I accidentally shot in air combat in the year 1918. I cannot live with that memory.

'You poor boy,' whispered Ellen Willmott to herself.

She picked up the pencil and started writing. It was a short note only, which she put next to the photograph before wrapping the oilskin back round.

'Is everything in order Miss Ellen?'

She started and looked up.

'No, not really. The brickwork at the rear of this building was inadequately finished. Fetch some mortar and I will repair it myself.'

'I am surprised,' said Jacob. 'Alex did it himself and he was usually so meticulous.'

'Perhaps something disturbed him. Just fetch the mortar.'

Jacob disappeared while she pondered on what she was doing. Would anyone ever see the photograph before it rotted away, which it would do however well protected it was? Would they care if they did find it? Would it just go on a bonfire somewhere? Did it matter anyway?

Jacob reappeared with a bucket of mortar.

'Just put it down there Jacob.'

'Yes Miss Ellen.'

'Jacob.'

'Yes Miss Ellen?'

'Thank you.'

He smiled and went on his way.

She picked up the bucket, went back to the rear of the summer house and carefully placing the package, replaced the bricks and mortared them in securely.

Wiping her hands on her skirt she put the bucket back at the front of the building for someone to pick up later and moved on to the alpine garden.

From behind a rhododendron some distance away Jacob smiled in admiration.

'She might be a dragon, but she's a clever dragon,' he whispered to himself. 'How on earth did she find out where it was? Well, that's where it stays.'

25

Finding Charles

'What if someone comes?' whispered Susan.

'It's eight o'clock on Tuesday. The working party works on Mondays and the specialist group don't get here until about ten. Don't worry, we won't be disturbed.'

Susan still looked anxiously about as Donald stared at the back wall of the summer house.

'What do you think?' he asked.

She pushed a sapling aside and moved closer, her eyes roaming over the wall.

'There,' she said, pointing.

'Why there?'

'All the mortar is worse for wear, but that seems to me to have been done more neatly than the rest. There's no mortar on the face of the bricks at all. It looks as though someone as careful as Alex might have done it.'

'Worth a try, anyway,' agreed Donald. 'I had no idea.'

He started chipping, every so often stopping to listen just in case Frank and Ben did come early. Then suddenly one brick came loose and as he pulled it free he saw a package at the rear.

'You were right,' he said excitedly, chipping away with renewed effort at the other three bricks. Finally they too came loose and he extracted the thin parcel from its little niche. He opened it and pulled out a photograph, passing the wrapping to Susan.

He saw a sepia picture of a strikingly handsome young man with a beautiful woman standing in what looked as if it was a garden in a country estate. He turned it over and saw the names written there.

'He was Charles Everington,' he said, turning to Susan. But Susan was busy peeling a piece of notepaper from inside the wrapping.

'It's a note from Ellen Willmott,' she said. 'She must have found the hiding place. It says 'Charles was a wonderful man who cared too much.' It's signed 'Ellen Ann Willmott'. I just can't believe it!'

She passed the note to Donald, who read it for himself in silence.

'We really have to think about this,' said Donald. 'I don't know what to do.'

'Come on,' said Susan, taking him by the hand. 'Let's sit and talk about it for a minute.'

They walked on for a couple of minutes.

'We'd better not go too far in case we decide just to put it back,' said Donald. 'Let's sit here.'

He took off his coat and spread it on a rock near the gorge and they lowered themselves on to it.

'Alex really wanted it kept quiet,' started Donald. 'Perhaps we should respect that.'

'But the people involved are long since dead. He may have distant family that would like to know the truth.'

'But they think the truth is that he died in the war, just like millions of other poor souls, and died a hero. Why disillusion them?'

'Because they deserve to know the real truth.'

'But Ellen Willmott and Jacob Maurer are involved too. They obviously wanted to keep it quiet or they would have said something when he died.'

'Suicide was a crime in those days, and a sin. It's simply the sign of a tortured mind now but they would have seen it as bringing disgrace on the family.'

They lapsed into silence again.

'There is one overriding reason.'

'What's that?'

'I couldn't tell lies to the other volunteers. Neither could you. We must tell them and agree together what should be done.'

'What should be done about what?'

They spun round to see half a dozen people behind them.

'Sorry to startle you,' continued Daphne. 'Monthly specialist group? We come round on the last Tuesday of every month to check on the flora?'

'Oh, sorry, I forgot the time. Hello Ben, hi Frank.'

'You probably don't know Deirdre and Sally then,' said Daphne. 'This is Donald, a recent volunteer. And I'd guess you are his lovely wife?'

'Yes, sorry, we were just chatting.'

'We have something to say. Something important.'

They were on their feet now, Susan nodding in agreement.

'Just look at that,' Deirdre broke in suddenly. 'I've never noticed that before. *Primula sikkimensis*, I'm sure, several of them just coming up next to the rock. I'll have to check, it's very late for it to flower and it likes damp soil, but it certainly looks like it. Are you two all right?'

' *Primula sikkimensis*,' Susan said to Donald. 'Wasn't that the flower that Alex first learned about?'

'Yes, it was.'

'Alex? Who is Alex?' asked Daphne.

'I have a confession to make,' explained Donald. 'The very day I started here I found some loose bricks in the wall in the walled garden. When I pulled them out to clean them before mortaring them back I found a notebook. It was difficult to read so I took it home and managed to decipher it, with a bit of guesswork. I put it on my computer and printed it out, meaning to give it to you straight away. It was the journal of a man who worked here for a short time in 1919. He was an ex-pilot and he killed himself. It's more complicated than that, but that was the essence of it.'

'Ellen Willmott and Jacob Maurer hushed it up - for his sake, not theirs,' continued Susan.

Donald carried on. 'He didn't want his true identity known, for reasons given in his journal. But he couldn't bring himself to hide it for ever, so he left a photograph and his name hidden. He left a clue leading us to where it was hidden. Susan solved it yesterday and we came here early to see if she was right.'

'And you have it there?' asked Deirdre.

'Yes,' said Donald, handing over the package containing the photograph. 'There is a short note from Ellen Willmott in there too. She must have solved the clue as well, but after looking at the photograph put it back where it was.'

'And here is the journal,' said Susan, opening her bag and pulling out a bulging brown envelope.

Deirdre took it.

The others crowded round while she first looked at the photograph, then at the note. Then she carefully opened the journal amidst gasps from the others.

'Sorry,' said a contrite Donald meekly.

'Sorry? What for?' said Ben.

'For not giving it to you as soon as we had found it.'

'If you'd done that we might never have found the photograph.'

'This ought to go to the Essex Record Office,' said Steve.

'No, not yet,' Donald broke in firmly. 'Read it first. I can print out copies of the transcript to avoid damaging the original. But there are reasons why Alex didn't want his true identity known. We might want to abide by his wishes.'

'That seems reasonable,' said Frank. 'After all, it's been there for over eighty years, a few more days won't matter.'

'I'll get them printed out and with you in the next few days,' said Donald.

'Can I borrow the original?' asked Deirdre.

Donald nodded his agreement.

'There's one further thing,' he said. 'According to Jacob Maurer's note at the back of the Journal, they buried him by the alpine garden. They put a rock over his grave. And Jacob planted *Primula sikkimensis* round it.'

They all looked at the rock on which Donald and Susan had been sitting, and at the flowers growing when and where they shouldn't be.

No-one said a word.

26

Resolution

Donald put down his chipping hammer and picked up his rucksack as he heard the whistle blow for tea break.

'Oh, that was well timed,' said Carla, trowelling the last of her mortar between two bricks.

They met Ben coming the opposite way as they made for the display area, followed by a puzzled looking Susan.

'We're having it by the bridge today,' explained Ben.

'How's it going?' Donald asked Susan, falling in beside her.

'I'm enjoying it, really glad I came. Finding balsam is more difficult than I thought but pulling it up isn't a problem. The nettles are though!'

She rubbed her arms ruefully.

They reached the chestnuts and turned towards the bridge where someone had dragged some benches.

Donald rummaged in his bag and found a banana and bottle of water.

'Nice to have you with us,' Gordon said to Susan, delighted at the change in their attitude to each other.

'It's good to be here.'

'Hello all.'

Donald looked up. Four people had come over the bridge, two he knew, two he didn't. An old but upright woman, walking with a stick that seemed more for show than necessity, and a middle aged man carrying what looked like a rather heavy briefcase.

'Hello Frank. Hello Deirdre. Special tour then?' said Donald.

'Sort of. Donald, Susan – Deirdre pointed to them both in turn – meet Olivia and Charles Henderson.'

Donald choked on his banana and Susan froze, before both recovering and getting to their feet.

'Sorry Donald, sorry Susan,' explained Frank. 'But I think we more or less agreed that we would try to trace the family.'

'Yes, but I had no idea it could be done this quickly. I'm glad though,' he added hastily.

'What Charles never knew was that Olivia had a daughter,' said Olivia. 'She was my mother.'

'So you are – '

'Yes, Charles' daughter.' She laughed. 'My mother told me they had a rather passionate time together the evening before he went back to France. Calling me Olivia as well has caused a bit of confusion, but never mind. Anyway, when I got married and had a son, I called him Charles, in memory of my father.'

'Your mother must have been devastated to lose her fiancée and her brother at the same time. Have you…'

'Read the journal? Yes, I have.' Her eyes saddened. 'He thought he had killed Harry.'

'Well he did, didn't he?'

'No, he didn't,' broke in Charles as his mother's eyes closed and her head bowed. 'The family wanted to know what happened and spoke to the C.O. of his squadron, but he only knew – or thought he knew – that they had both been killed in an air battle. When the war was over we managed to trace one of the Germans involved in that fight. It was he who was diving on and shooting at Harry's plane when Charles somehow found himself between them. The German is absolutely sure that it was his bullets that struck Harry and then Charles.'

Donald was thunderstruck. Susan clutched at his hand.

'So poor Charles' heartache, his memory loss, his death – they were all for nothing?'

'It would seem so.'

Donald felt his throat close and his eyes watering. Susan was dabbing her eyes by his side.

'Sorry, we really felt we had got to know him transcribing his journal and trying to imagine what he was like.'

Olivia went up to them both and put her arms round them for a minute.

'Everyone who met him seemed to find him a wonderful man,' said Daphne. 'Even Ellen Willmott.'

'I suppose that's what makes it so tragic,' murmured Deirdre.

'Do you know where he is buried?' asked Charles.

'Not for certain,' said Donald. 'But we do know a rock covered his grave and that some felt it was sort of out of place with the general layout. It was also planted with *Primula sikkimensis.*'

'What do they look like?'

Deirdre pointed to the plants round the base of the rock. About half a metre high, with clusters of funnel shaped yellow flowers hanging down, they were bold but not spectacularly beautiful flowers. 'They look just like those, but we've never seen them there before and it's very late in the season for them to be flowering. It's not one of your jokes, is it Gordon?'

Gordon shook his head.

'So this is where my grandfather's body lies?' said Charles.

'Probably.'

'And no-one else knows?'

'No.'

'I've read his journal too now. He was really happy here. That sounds silly when he killed himself, but that was nothing to do with Warley Place. If we exhume him the whole sad story will come out and probably end up in the tabloids. Can we leave him here?'

'I think I can say it's perfectly all right with us,' said Frank. 'In fact we too could do without that sort of publicity.'

There were nods of agreement all round.

'You've closed a chapter for us,' said Olivia. 'We always wondered why his body could never be found. Is there anything we can do for you? Would money help?'

'Well the Trust can always do with more funds,' said Frank. 'But really we are content here. Sometimes we wonder if we should restore small parts of the garden to the state it was when Ellen Willmott was alive, just to give a flavour as it were. But do it too well and we'll find vandals coming in and stealing the plants or breaking anything we build. Anyway, it's a nature reserve, not a garden. So really we think we are best leaving it as it is, restoring the brickwork, keeping weeds at bay and making it safe for occasional visitors. That way it retains its magic, too.'

'We're collecting archive material,' said Steve. 'But again, if we make any sort of museum here, however small, it will get broken into.'

'I can see that,' said Charles. 'What a pity. We'd like to thank you in some way, and I'm sure we can think of something. Meanwhile, perhaps you two would accept a little gift from us both – and from my grandfather.'

160

He handed the briefcase over to Donald who almost dropped it when the weight became apparent. He put it on the rock and opened it. There were two books inside.

'*The Genus Rosa!*' he gasped. 'How on earth did you get a copy? It's too much, we can't accept this!'

The others crowded round looking as he gingerly turned a few pages.

'It was our own copy,' said Olivia. 'We have quite an extensive library. We can replace it, given a little time. And we won't accept no for an answer, we would be most upset if you refused it.'

'Well when you get another copy let us know and we can exchange it for your own original,' suggested Susan.

'Thank you, we may well do that.'

'This is a happy place now,' said Susan.

'It certainly is,' agreed Donald. He turned to Olivia. 'Susan and I were here a month or so ago and we were scared witless by David's alarm system. Ellen Willmott used to have tripwires set up to deter thieves at night and David and Frank set up a modern equivalent that made it sound like Miss Willmott's ghost warning people off when it was dark. Then when we were here one night a week ago, right on this spot, we heard a sigh. But it was a happy sigh, as if everything was all right now. The whole atmosphere changed.'

'Probably the wind,' said David.

'No, it was definitely a sort of 'ah' sound, not wind and not a bird or an animal. How did you do it?'

'I didn't,' said David. 'The system is back in my workshop getting fixed. A squirrel must have got up there and chewed the wires off. It hasn't worked for at least a fortnight.'

Appendices

Appendices in a novel? Well this is more than a novel and you may well want to know more about Ellen Willmott, Warley Place and the work done there by Essex Wildlife Trust. If you do, these appendices may provide a taster for further exploration.

Appendix 1   Bibliography.

Appendix 2.   Biographies.

Appendix 3.   Warley Place now.

Appendix 4.   Warley Place in 1919.

Appendix 1
Bibliography

Miss Willmott of Warley Place by Audrey le Lievre.
This book is no longer in print but is available from the public library and is well worth reading. It provided much of the background information for *The Wall*.

Warley Magna to Great Warley by George Harper.
This book is also an excellent reference source, both for Warley Place and for the wider history of the locality. It is also available in the public library.

Warley Place
This well illustrated Essex Wildlife Trust booklet is an excellent guide to the people, the fauna and the flora of Warley Place.

Appendix 2
Biographies

Ellen Willmott

Ellen Ann Willmott was born in 1858 and with her father, mother and sister Rose moved to Warley Place in 1875. She had always had a keen interest in gardening and following the death of her parents and the marriage of her sister (later, sadly, her death) she ran the estate on her own.

She was a very wealthy woman, her money partly handed down from her own father and partly given to her by her godmother.

She had many interests apart from gardening. She had some very expensive musical instruments and was a good violinist and choral singer. She was a photographer and her book *Warley Place in Spring and Summer* (which can be viewed in Brentwood Library) contains a number of her photographs. She also had her own lathe, printing press and telescope. But it was gardening that was her overriding passion and she developed a garden that was second to none.

Although the First World War did not help matters, the truth is that she spent too much money both on Warley Place and her estates in Italy and France. By the end of the war she struggled from one financial crisis to the next and her death in 1934 mercifully happened before she finally would have had to sell Warley Place.

She was a remarkable woman.

James Robinson

James Robinson started work for the Willmott family in 1890 and served until Ellen Willmott's death. He developed from the butler to someone who ran the house and became her confidant. He was rewarded by the gift of The Red House in which he was able to live out what few years he had left.

Jacob Maurer

Ellen Willmott 'poached' Jacob Maurer from his Swiss employer in 1894. He was a quiet man and dedicated to the development of the Alpine Garden, although as things became more difficult and the number of gardeners diminished he had to spread his energies a little further.

He lived in South Lodge, eventually with his wife Rosina and nine children. When you look at South Lodge you wonder how they were all squeezed in! Sadly his wife died in 1918 of tuberculosis. He later married the daughter of the woman who ran the bothy.

He stayed at Warley Place until it was sold on Ellen Willmott's death, then moved to Billericay but died in 1937 in his native Switzerland.

Appendix 3

Warley Place as it is now

This map and the accompanying notes, from which the events related in the book can be located, have been taken from the Essex Wildlife Trust Warley Place Trail Guide, suitably abbreviated to suit the text.

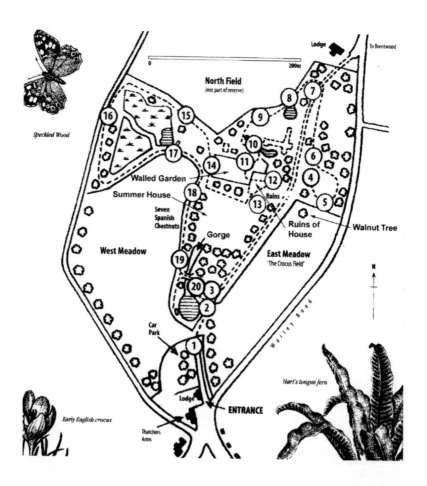

The aim of the Trust at Warley Place is to improve the different habitats for the benefit of the wildlife while retaining those parts of the garden that have survived.

Warley Place is open to members of Essex Wildlife Trust or to other members of the public by appointment. Please keep to the footpaths. Some parts of the reserve are dangerous because of hidden cellars and decaying walls.

The numbers below are those appearing on the marker posts on the walk round the reserve.

1. On the left as you enter the gate is the old lodge in which Jacob Maurer and his family lived. The drive from the gate to the car park borders the crocus field (East Meadow), which, in spring, used to be a sea of purple flowers. Some crocuses can still be seen in the field and in the border to the drive, but most do not now flower, apparently because of grazing by rabbits. This is one of the few sites in Britain where the early English crocus grows naturally.

2. The South Pond is all that remains of the medieval water point for Great Warley village. The main coloniser is common reed, but yellow flag and marsh marigold are among other water plants. The path from the car park to the stile and on through the reserve was the drive to the house and before that the main road from Great Warley to Brentwood. The road was moved to its present position in the 19th century.

3. In late winter, snowdrops of many varieties can be seen bordering the path. Near the top of the slope, on the left, is where the house stood until it was demolished in 1939; the turning circle is still visible. Opposite, on the right, a ha-ha borders the crocus field. The ditch and wall kept grazing cattle out of the garden without the need for a hedge, which would have blocked the view. In the meadow stands the walnut tree dating from Ellen Willmott's time.

4. Notice the remains of the coach house on the left. There is a barrier across the old drive here and two smaller paths lead off to

the right through the old orchard area and rockery. Beyond the barrier is 'the butterfly ride', an open area with flowering shrubs and nettles to attract butterflies. Taking the path to the right leads through a patch of Abraham, Isaac and Jacob *Trachystemon orientalis*, another relic of Miss Willmott's time.

5. In spring and summer the characteristic smell of onions at this point indicates ransoms or wild garlic which is well established. Other plants include *Corydalis*, hart's tongue ferns and meadow saffron.

6. This area was recently cleared of bamboo and bramble. The large tree on the right is a Tree of Heaven *Ailanthus*.

7. This was the main cold frame area of the garden. Following the removal of sycamores and ivy, many attractive flowers appear each year.

8. The artificial pond was a reservoir for watering the cold frames and greenhouses. The site of the group of greenhouses can be seen from the plan attached to the rail.

9. The ivy-covered stump on the right was a sycamore that lived for about 140 years. It was used as a resting point for tawny owls until the top fell off.

10. Next to the nursery is a narrow half-moon shaped pond and beyond it a brick-sided reservoir similar to the one at post 8.

11. The walled garden probably dates from the 17th century, but much of it is the result of Miss Willmott's planting. There is a fine ginkgo tree, a few magnolias and a palm. A considerable amount of work is being done to repair the wall which in places was in poor condition.

12. The house was demolished in 1939 and much of the ground floor has fallen into the cellars. Mosaic flooring can be seen in places. The small building now used as an information room and a tea-room for volunteers was a cloakroom and WC. A variety of ferns flourish in the cellar.

13. The conservatory was part of the house and still stands, though without a roof or glazing. Its mosaic floor is raised so that tepid water could be stored beneath. The large window leads out to what was the lawn and bowling green. The building was in a dangerous condition but has recently been stabilised to make it safe for people to enter.

14. From the terrace, which is currently being restored, there was a clear view of the lakes at the bottom of the slope.

15. Bluebells can be seen on the left and the two large trees on the right are a large turkey oak and a Caucasian wing-nut.

16. The lower tree-covered area was the bog garden and a concrete-edged boating lake. The lake floor now hardly shows so much as a puddle, even in the wettest weather. At the far end there is the wall of the old boat house with a rail still in position.

17. The hide overlooks the North Pond, which is reputed to have been a carp pond when the estate belonged to the nuns of Barking Abbey.

18. The Spanish or sweet chestnuts were reputed to have been planted by the diarist John Evelyn in the 17th century. On the left is the partly restored old summer house.

19. The large beech tree on the left was planted about 1810, but the top had to be cut off to render it safe. Along the spur to the hide overlooking South Pond can be seen patches of purple toothwort.

20. The bridge spans the gorge which Miss Willmott had constructed as part of her Alpine Garden. The rocks were brought from Yorkshire. The remains of the filmy fern cave can be seen from here.

Appendix 4
Warley Place as it was

This map of Warley Place, taken with kind permission from the Essex Wildlife Trust booklet *Warley Place*, actually relates to the year 1904 but should be sufficient for the purposes of this book.

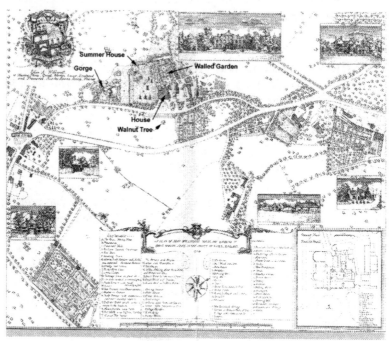

A Plan of Miss Willmott's House and Gardens at Great Warley 1904